CAUGHT BY THE KINGPIN

EVIE ROSE

Copyright © 2023 by Evie Rose

All rights reserved.

No part of this book may be reproduced in any form or by any electronic or mechanical means, including information storage and retrieval systems, without written permission from the author, except for the use of brief quotations in a book review.

This story is a work of fiction. Names, characters, places, and incidents are the product of the author's imagination or are used fictitiously. Any resemblance to actual events, locales, or persons, living or dead, is coincidental.

Cover: © 2024 by Evie Rose. Images under licence from Deposit Photos.

❦ Created with Vellum

1

FELICITY

I dread my phone ringing. Not just because messages are much more civilised, though that's definitely the case. It's so intrusive to make someone's phone yell at them until they talk to you. A message ping doesn't necessitate panicked handwashing when you're in the middle of a messy baking moment and have eggy fingers, butter smeared on your forehead, and flour on your boobs.

What? I had an itch.

No, I dread my phone ringing because invariably it is my father making a demand from the next room, when he could just get up.

"Whisky," he barks. "And tea for my guest."

Not sure if his orders would be better via message, actually. Maybe semaphore?

As I put the kettle on, clean myself up, and pull out the fancy cut-glass decanter with the whisky, I feel kinship with the guest. One sniff of my father's clear beige nail varnish remover—sorry, whisky—makes me want to barf. It's not even as though my father really likes it. When I swap out the expensive bottles for the stuff on special offer, he doesn't notice the difference. A lack of taste that will ultimately lose him his little slave: me.

There was a short time when I looked forward to messages on my phone. I did beta reading of romance novels to make money towards one of my first escape attempts, and the buzz as a new smutty story arrived, or an author thanking me for my comments, made my heart fill with helium.

Finding all my earnings stolen was how I discovered my father taps my phone. My father called it "rent" when I asked him, and had one of his goons punch me in the stomach when I complained.

I try not to complain anymore.

They're in the grandest of the reception rooms, all gaudy old uncomfortable furniture and paintings of sludgy landscapes in gilded frames. The man my father is talking at has his back to me. His curly cropped hair is so black it has a sheen of blue as well as flecks of silver and his broad shoulders are encased in a fine grey wool suit that I know without touching would be warm.

My father's shoulders are by his ears, uncharacteristically tense for a mafia boss. He ignores me as I start to unload the tray onto the low table between him and the unknown man.

"This is an excellent investment opportunity. I would prefer to keep it for myself, but some of my capital is tied up at the moment."

I manage not to snort with derision as I place the cups and saucers. Tied up? Yeah. His money is very tied up with the Westminster mafia he owes money to. This man will be fleeced if he invests. Probably deserves it though, he'll be a mean old mafioso like the rest of—

I glance across to the man my father is attempting to con, and I'm caught.

His eyes. They're light blue and staring into me. Not over my head, or examining my chest with idle speculation. He's looking at me as though he can strip away my outward appearance and these shapeless dark clothes and see the swirls of pink and green and blue I imagine make up my soul. As though he can see stars in my drab, colourless eyes and a rainbow in my brown hair. This man looks at my plain appearance and freckled cheeks like I'm an oasis after weeks in the desert. Like I'm beautiful.

Which I've been told repeatedly, I'm not.

But *him*, he's utterly compelling.

Not handsome, exactly. Nothing like the slick and preening young men who work for the Kensington mafia, with their designer clothes and smooth jaws. Nope. This man looks exactly like what he is: a powerful and ruthless mafia boss. Broad shoulders, muscled thighs, a light smattering of hair at the wrists exposed by crisp white cuffs. Strong and dangerous and gruff and... Kind? I'm probably making that last bit up, but his eyes are more summer morning sky than winter glacier. Although his hair is salt and pepper, the stubble on his jaw is black, and a thin curved scar runs across his cheek.

He knows about pain, this man.

"Interesting." The man's voice is rough and low, lightly accented. Italian maybe? He flicks his gaze dismissively to my father, then returns to me. "Tell me about the potential profits."

My neck creaks like I'm stone as I drag my eyes to my role. Anonymous maid serving drinks.

My father begins a long and deliberately confusing

explanation of his con. He's sweating and nervous, trying to sound authoritative but this man has him rattled.

The man is dominant. There's no other word. The strongest of a pack of wolves, with his light eyes. It's not his house, but he's utterly at ease. He leans back, and for a second I'm self-centred enough that I think it's so he can see me from the corner of his eye as I finish transferring the contents of the tray to the table.

I pour out exactly two fingers of whisky for my father and while he gulps half of it down, I ask, "Would you like milk and sugar, sir?"

"Marco."

I blink and almost say we don't have any of that. But his *name*. Oh gosh that sinks into me all the way to the bone. Marco is exactly the right name for him. Straightforward and blunt, but also rich and lyrical.

"Marco." I bite my lip and nod to prevent myself from repeating his name to myself again and again. It replays in my head anyway. *Marco.*

Then the significance hits me. A mafia boss. Called Marco.

Marco Brent.

I go still. Even I have heard of the kingpin of the Brent mafia. Dangerous. Secretive. Powerful. Obscenely wealthy. Marco Brent is a bogeyman, head of the most discreet, subtle mafia of London. Brent is whispered in fear and respect by my father's henchmen.

"Milk, no sugar. Thank you...?"

"Felicity," I squeak as I pour the milk with shaking hands.

A grunt of disapproval comes from the other side of the table as my gaze meets Marco's and there's a ghost of a smile around his mouth as he takes the tea I offer, murmuring, "Thank you, Felicity."

I know it means happiness, but I've never felt any joy at people saying my name. It generally means there's washing up to do or someone needs a three-course meal in forty minutes' time.

But Marco saying my name... that does feel like happiness. Fizzing, popping, laughter and spinning around, bright-coloured exhilaration. I should be scared, but being regarded by Marco is how I imagine it feels to be wrapped in a sun-warmed towel after a cool, invigorating swim in a clear green-blue ocean. A shiver of heat and comfort, the scent of salt.

"As I was saying," my father continues with his pitch.

Marco takes me in as I stand, pale blue gaze dragging slowly up from my sensible black shoes, bare calves, shapeless knee-length black dress in a scratchy material I've never quite identified, to my face. I fight the urge not to fidget as he regards my hair, pulled back into a neat French braid. I can feel that a dark strand has come loose, as my soft flyaway hair often does, and is lying untidily across my cheek.

He follows the movement of my hand as I sweep the tendril behind my ear with something hungry in his expression.

That focus on me is... I can't remember anyone making me feel so special. There's a connection between us. It is as instant and undeniable as water into icing sugar. However rich he is, I don't want Marco to end up in the twenty-minutes-too-long-in-the-oven cake that my father is preparing.

"Would you like a cupcake?" I blurt out just as my

father says, "The gross capital gain will have compound interest and make crypto look like peanuts."

My father goes red in the face. "That won't—"

Marco cuts him off. "I'd love one of your cupcakes."

I snatch up the tray and rush out.

"There's no need to humour her," my father says in a carrying voice. "Thinks she's something special because her mother was my whore—"

I shut the door and take the labyrinthine route to the kitchen. I don't allow myself to think as I place yesterday's baking onto a tray. I rifle through the cupboards until I find my father's favourite decorations—gold powder—and sprinkle it over a few of the cakes with delicately piped buttercream and icing butterflies.

Is that clear? I hope so. I add a bit more.

My father is still speaking as I enter. The massive silver tray is tricky to juggle with the doors, but I chose it because it's too big to hold for long and might draw Marco away from my father so I can warn him.

Marco looks over as I place the tray onto a table on the other side of the room, well away from where they're sitting.

"Will you come and choose?" Please let my father be typically lazy.

"Just bring two over here," my father grunts. "We have urgent business to discuss."

Ahhggg. That'll spoil everything.

"Yes, sir." He likes it when I call him sir. Makes him feel superior or something.

"I'll choose myself." Marco's lip curls and he stands with deliberate slowness. His eyes flash cold and he strolls over to the tray of cakes, and lounges, one hand in his pocket. No hurry.

I pick up one of the gold cakes with plenty of icing, and

scuttle over to my father, placing it on a plate for him. He scowls and gives me a look I know means, *You're pushing your luck.*

One day I'll leave here and open a bakery. I'll make my talent for making cakes into a legitimate company so successful it'll make my father's mafia enterprise look like the failing forgot-the-eggs cake it is. As incompetent as it is illegal.

After all, he hasn't realised in over six months that I've been slowly skimming off money from the grocery budget via the special offers that provide cash back rather than a discount. Despite calling me into his office and examining each item on the receipt every week, he doesn't look at what really matters. He growls over things like cheap pyjamas, despite my actually needing new sleepwear. But he doesn't notice the pricey branded tinned tomatoes or sugar.

And every week I pocket the extra, saving for the day I will escape.

In the meantime, I'm going to help this terrifying, scarred kingpin who has shown me the kindness of looking at me rather than through me.

Marco has his face turned as though regarding the cakes, but is watching from the side of his eye as I walk back to him.

"They all look perfect," he says, but he is looking right at me, not the cakes. "I don't normally have a sweet tooth, but I'm tempted beyond belief by your... cake."

Pleasure skitters down my spine from the expression of unfettered desire on his face. Oh god why does he have to be a mob boss? Why can't he be a cupcake aficionado I meet when I'm set up in my new life?

"Don't choose that one." I point at one of the cakes I slathered in gold. "It's so pretty, but the decoration doesn't taste of anything. The plain-looking ones are better." There's no inflection in my phrase, and I've made the same comment many times, so no one listening would suspect. But does Marco understand what I mean?

His gaze lingers on my lips and my heart races.

"I agree. The overlooked ones are the sweetest."

But still, he's not looking at the cupcakes. He won't have noticed the cake I'm indicating is the *gold* one. The cake signifying wealth. The ones that are just a sheen of gold on top, but aren't as valuable as they seem.

I move to his side.

"You can't trust him," I whisper, the words tumbling out.

"Did you make these?" he says loud enough for my father to hear, then adds under his breath, "Are you in danger? Do you need help?"

From a kingpin? Because that worked out so well for my mother. Marco is gorgeous, yes, but I can't allow that to fool me.

"I made them all myself." I reply at normal volume, shaking my head, then add, "He owes money to Westminster."

The kingpin raises one eyebrow and the corner of his mouth hitches up. "That's quite a talent you have."

Yes, it is actually. No one takes any notice of me so they continue talking about confidential matters while I clear up their breakfast or serve afternoon tea. And for him to smirk? Pah.

"They shot the kneecaps from my father's second-in-command," I hiss.

"Uncivilised pigs." He adjusts his cuffs. "I'm sorry you had to see that."

We're talking in undertones, and it's a given that we're friends. I don't know why. But he trusts me and I trust him.

Because he saw you, a little voice pipes up. *He noticed you when you're invisible to everyone else.*

"If you ever decide to sell these cupcakes, let me know. I'd be happy to help." As he looks at me, heat flares over my skin, stealing my breath.

"Anytime," he adds, and it feels like a promise.

I nod and Marco finally casts a cursory glance over the cupcakes.

"This one is *mine*." He takes the simplest of the cupcakes; the one I would have chosen. White butter icing with a slice of strawberry on top. Elegant. He strips back the paper and bites.

A raw sound of enjoyment and appreciation comes from him as he chews. I stare unabashedly at his dark and bristly jawline. I wonder what it would feel like beneath my fingertips. He swallows and oh gosh, his throat. It's so strong and firm and I fight the urge to rub my thighs together. I'm flushed and more aware of the space between my legs than I ever have been before in my twenty years of life.

I glance across at my father, who is just finishing his cake, brushing crumbs from his chin.

Marco finishes his mouthful and pins me with that pale blue gaze again. "Delicious, cara. Thank you."

Cara. A sweet Italian endearment in his husky voice.

It probably means nothing. Just gratitude for having warned him off working with the Kensington mafia.

But the next batch of icing I make I'll be adding tiny drops of blue until I recreate the colour. The blue of his eyes.

"Don't stop baking," he murmurs as he walks away, back to my father. "I'll be back to claim *everything*."

2

MARCO

I sit back into the limo, my head reeling despite having endured sixty fucking minutes with that idiot Kensington after seeing Felicity.

For fifteen years I've been the head of the Brent mafia. I've quietly pulled it from obscurity compared to our famous London neighbours, first to acknowledgement, then discomfort, and finally respect and pure dark fear. In all that time, I've focused on my work and making a team I can rely on to carry out my orders. I've built an empire. But no one tells you the price. I don't think even I noticed until it was too late.

Being at the top of the pyramid, however solidly you've built it, is lonely. No one can touch me. That feeling has been my only constant companion, a pane of glass between me and the world. Protective, yes, but isolated.

The moment I saw Felicity, it shattered. I could feel her vibrancy, her determination, and the heat of her lush body. She's the sun revealing itself in a glorious rainbow after a long drizzly day.

Brave as well as gorgeous, such an angel, trying to warn

me about her father. Unnecessary, since I was only there to assess the extent of the financial problems at Kensington. I was never going to invest, but though I suspected Westminster's dirty tricks were involved, she saved me some questions by confirming that. My girl already knew where her loyalty lay: with me. But she's far gutsier than most women would be with a vindictive dickhead like Kensington, taking a risk talking back to him and putting her safety at risk to help me. And that trick with using the gold cupcakes to warn me off investing? Amazing. Subtle and witty and intelligent.

A whip-smart mind and perfect beauty hidden in plain sight. Big grey eyes, the colour of smoke and just as mysterious. I can't believe she's been overlooked all this time, as though all the men in Kensington knew she was mine and left her alone, waiting for me. The Kensington mafia are clearly ignorant misogynists, unaware of how this woman will be a powerful ally. Nimble and strong enough to break all my defences. I've never been bothered by younger women before. I prefer more experience and fewer expectations.

Felicity broke that idea. Pulverised it. I want her to ask things of me, and I want to be the man to introduce her to everything she wants in the world.

I can't believe it. After years of being alone, my heart demanded I claim her the instant our gazes met. Along with my cock it was the leader of a fuck coup against my brain, and they threaten to lead my whole body to do something animalistic. It took all my self-control not to just take her the moment I saw her.

Thankfully I managed to simply take a sip of tea, like a good British psychopath should, repressing all my Italian fire, and swear she'd be mine.

I've never believed in fate. I make my own luck, I don't wait around for anything. But Felicity? I think maybe meeting her was some sort of magic. Destiny.

She felt it too, I'm certain. The only reason I'm leaving without her slung over my shoulder is because of that shake of her head.

I'll have to wait. There will be hours and days until she's by my side again. It makes my teeth ache.

Will she be as sweet as one of her cupcakes when I lick her out? I bet she'll be even more delicious. Sweet and salt and moaning as I make her come.

There are a hundred ways I'm going to give her pleasure. On my fingers, my tongue, my cock. With her naked and grinding onto my face, using my mouth, and at my mercy, tied up while I pleasure her again and again until she begs me to make her mine.

My cock is so fucking hard, and I wish I had a photo of her to look at. CCTV. I'll find footage. I'll discover everything about her, and grant her every wish. But right now...

"Circle around for a bit," I order the driver before flicking the switch to close the screen between us.

I barely wait until it's shut before I fumble with my belt, the clink loud in my ears, and rip open my flies. My cock pokes up, and it's half a second to shove my boxers down and expose it.

I close my eyes and think of Felicity as I grasp my cock and fist it hard. I can't wait to see her dark hair spilling over my pillow. I wonder how far those cute freckles extend?

My cock is leaking with how much I need release, and although part of me wants to wait until I'm with her, I'll go mad without relief.

I've never wanted kids before, but as soon as I think of

being with Felicity naked, it's right. I'll breed her. She'll be rounded with our child. Ripe and even more desirable.

My thoughts are soft, but my actions are rough. Brutal even. I hate that I need this, that it's not her hand on my cock. Or her wet heat sheathing me and milking out my orgasm into her body as she comes on my cock. So I do what I have to in order to sate the bodily need I feel after seeing her.

"Felicity." I choke out her name as I come, and the memory of her face makes the sharp wash of pleasure a release and an ache.

Cleaning up and tucking myself away, my skin prickles.

This was wrong. She should be here, with me. I should be licking her pussy and taking care of her, and I'm left with an overwhelming instinct to return to her.

I thought an orgasm thinking of my girl would take the edge off. Maybe make it easier to think rationally.

It hasn't.

I'm worse. More obsessed. I don't think I can do this again—touch myself—until we're together. That pleasure was empty without her, a shell of the satisfaction I'd have sinking into her welcoming pussy. I scrape my hand over my face and through my hair, my frustration worse than it was before.

Feeling this dirty might have to be something I get used to.

At thirty-nine, I'm probably twice her age.

She's tiny and pure, sweet and innocent. I'm amoral, scarred, and probably going to destroy her family.

She's also strong and clever. The only reason a girl like her says she doesn't need any help when she's obviously in a shitty situation is because she's cooking up a way out. I hope there are no men involved, because they'll have an untimely death if they touch my girl.

I'll be watching every moment, protecting her. Life has dealt her a poor hand so far, but from this point onwards, that changes. She's about to become very lucky. I'll discover all the things she wants most in the world, and give them to her along with all the love and orgasms she can take. That sadness I saw in her grey eyes? I'll remove every cause, including her father.

I won't stop until Felicity is happy.

From today, I have a new job. The whole of Brent's considerable forces will be focused on one person. Felicity. And one task.

Operation *Wife*.

3

FELICITY

Since Marco, I've been living in a mirror. It all looks the same, but feels totally different.

Narrowing it down, the change is three things.

First, my whole body has decided to vibrate. Not literally, I'm not having a stroke. But my nipples tingle and my pussy gets warm whenever the vision of Marco's face appears in my mind. That's honestly, like eighty per cent of the time, because cooking, cleaning, and planning escape aren't particularly exciting.

Along with that, the dull fear that has accompanied me for years, probably since my mother "disappeared" when I was eleven after a particularly angry argument with my father, has lifted. I've been scheming this latest escape for months, and if I'm honest with myself, putting it off to avoid another disappointment and punishment.

But since Marco's visit, I'm confident. I can do this. A big scary creature saw something compelling in me, and that knowledge makes me believe I'll succeed.

The third invisible change is how it feels to be watched.

Anyone involved with the mafia is always being observed. Suspicion is the stock in trade, and I'm used to all the little ways of hiding myself and what I'm doing. And that's still present, don't get me wrong. But there's another layer now, a warm protection.

I guess it's just the satisfaction of having outwitted my father—he thought I was just showing off my baking skills. For once, the punishment burn on my arm doesn't hurt that much. I run my finger down the pale scars from previous infractions, and I think of that scar on Marco's cheek. The similarity is a line of connection, a pale link. The same feeling as being watched over, guarded.

I'm probably imagining things.

It's been four days and it seems like a dream when I remember him. His pale blue eyes. That grey suit. The scent of the ocean when I stood next to him.

Every night, I think of Marco and, dream or not, the wetness between my legs and the squirming need that makes me shift in my narrow bed is real. I touch myself and come to a silent, shuddering release, my body washed with relief after a whole day of turning myself inside out with wanting him. I stroke myself in the dark of night in my bedroom and think of his deep voice and his words.

I'll be back to claim everything.

What will he claim?

I guess it doesn't matter. I finally counted the cash I've been saving up and allowed myself to believe I could get away. Less than a month and I'll have enough money to leave and I won't see Marco again, even if he did return to claim... me.

I'd be far away, starting my new life in Scotland.

I chose Scotland for three reasons. One, it's as far from

London as you can go and still be in the same country. Important consideration, since I don't have a passport.

Two. The best strawberries come from Scotland. Raspberries too. The sweetest, plumpest, best fruit that I use to decorate my cupcakes, arrives from the north. They're always gorgeously red on the inside, like the lipstick Mum used to wear. Got to be a good place if they have strawberry farms, right? At a pinch, I could always work on one if I can't make my bakery work.

I will, though.

And three is a bit silly. Romantic, especially for the daughter of a... But in my favourite historical romance book the handsome hero sweeps the heroine off to Gretna Green, just over the border into Scotland, to marry her against her father's wishes.

Obviously I don't have any illusions about anyone wanting to marry me. Nah, not going to happen. I'll be on my own, as I always am, but... I dunno. I want to run to Scotland so I can imagine I'm going to Gretna Green with a man so passionately in love with me he's defying family and convention to marry me. I'm going to Scotland because it's a place to build the life your heart desires.

It's all planned out and the bank notes hidden, rolled into the seams of my favourite old hoody. It will be a long road to my dreams, and even then, I'll still be alone. No scandalously flirting with a Regency duke, marriage at Gretna Green, orgasms, babies, and a husband to love me.

The love bit is probably the most unlikely part of all that, including a duke from the Regency. I'm not very lovable. People like my cupcakes, even if everyone here has an opinion about whether they're too sweet, moist, dry, or have too little decoration or too much. However hard I try, I'm not lovable.

Marco Brent won't come for me. No one ever has. So I breathe deeply, tell myself escape to Scotland will be enough, and fall asleep into a sea of pale blue.

A visit to the supermarket is a red-letter day. Even before I started saving up, I loved going to the supermarket. I get to look at things and fantasise about buying whatever I want. And no one follows me around. So far as my father is concerned, shopping is a menial task that I do and he merely has to check the receipt for anything illicit.

Like, you know. Clothes. Chocolate bars. He grumbles every time he sees period stuff on the bill, like I'm inconsiderate to bleed every month.

I suggested four years ago when I'd just turned sixteen, that if he didn't want the expense of keeping me around he should allow me to leave. His mouth made an ugly line. He said that if I was more costly than useful, he'd take me up on that offer and I'd leave in bin bags.

On balance I prefer all my limbs attached and in old pyjamas. I think that suits me better.

Hence the need for this convoluted plan and careful use of supermarket trips.

Today, it's a bit different. I think I'm sensing a ghost? A nice one that accompanies me to the supermarket?

I have this weird tingle over my neck and scalp, and I keep almost seeing someone out of the corner of my eye. But when I look, they're gone.

Probably I'm just so starved of positive interactions that my mind is playing tricks.

I indulge in browsing the paperbacks. I limit my imaginary purchases to three, and dither over the third book.

They're historical romances. Two are my favourite authors, a dead cert, but should I have the one with a duke who's a spy, or a marriage of convenience with a rake? I read the blurbs and check the prices and the relative length and focus as though I'm actually going to purchase any of them.

I'm not.

In the end I go for the duke spy. Powerful and dangerous book boyfriends, who can resist, right? I hold the three books in my hands and imagine taking them home, putting them on my bed, and reading them until they're tattered and dog-eared. I sniff the spines for that paper smell. Then I put all the books back into their correct place on the shelf, for someone else to read.

It's only when I'm unpacking the shopping that I find the duke book.

It's tucked between two bags of sugar. And much as I try to think how it could have happened accidentally, they're all just as implausible as a poltergeist.

It was a ghost. My ghost.

I won't be able to take much with me, so the next week I look at the jewellery in the store-within-a-store. Again, just to dream.

There's a locked cabinet with expensive rings and necklaces. I stare through the glass and imagine the weight of the metal on my finger, or over my clavicle.

I press my nose up to the cool glass and admire the way the diamond sparkles on the big engagement ring, holding my hand out and trying to see what it would look like on me.

Two more supermarket trips and I'll have enough money saved.

There's increased tension at home. Westminster are making bleak threats about what they'll do if they aren't paid soon. From that I assume Marco hasn't fallen for my father's scheme, and although I ought to be nervous about my family's finances, I'm only relieved Marco won't lose out.

I find the ring in a bag of cherries I don't remember buying.

Exactly the one I'd been looking at. The most expensive ring in the display.

Not a ghost, but a man.

A thief? For me?

I'm heated all over that someone cares enough to give me this ring, because it's no accident. And though I've never seen him, I know the feel of this man's attention and it is the most consideration I've had in years.

Subtle too, not putting me in danger from my father. It's like I've been given invisible armour. Someone values me, albeit anonymously.

I secret the ring into the right cuff of my hoody, but I can't resist bringing it out and looking at it every night. I slip it onto my fourth finger and imagine a duke gave me it because he wants to marry me.

A duke with pale blue eyes, salt and pepper hair, and a scar down the side of his face.

This is the last time I'll buy my father's groceries, and see my ghost. I choose a greeting card that says *Thank You* and prop it open, sticking up out of the shelves. I know he's watching.

In the next aisle, I browse kitchenware for a few minutes, unable to concentrate on the bowls in soft blues and greens that I usually love. I'm eager to get back to the greeting cards, but I don't want to scare him off. I sneak looks out of the corner of my eye.

A middle-aged woman with a baby. A young guy in a T-shirt who walks past makes me blink, but no. I don't think that's my stalker. Then a tall shadow of a dark suit and a flash of blue eyes. So smooth and fast, by the time my brain has caught up and I've turned, he's gone. I rush to the end of the aisle, and then look down the next, and the next, almost sprinting.

Where is he? Marco. Was that...?

But he's nowhere to be found. Holding in the scream of frustration is like shutting an overflowing fizzy pop bottle. All the disappointment is there, waiting to spill over the moment I open the cap.

It wasn't Marco.

Kingpins do not go around leaving presents for girls they met once. Maybe it *was* a ghost.

With heavy feet scuffing the smooth floor, I walk back to my trolley.

I almost don't return to the card section, but go out of duty. Should put the card in its correct slot, right? No need to make more work for the shop assistants.

Where I put the thank-you card, there's another replacing it. It's red and white. Simple and baffling.

It's designed to look like a playing card: the queen of hearts. It reads, *And I'm playing for keeps.*

I huff in irritation even as delight tingles under my ribs.

But it's over. Next week I'm putting my plan into action.

When I get back home and I'm unloading the shopping, I tell myself I'm not expecting anything, because how can he top the ring from last week? And maybe I imagined the whole thing. Among the other confectionery, making me doubt whether I bought them myself, is something I've never had.

A bag of Hershey's kisses.

I smuggle them up to my bedroom and suck each one. I relish the chocolate as it melts in my mouth.

And I try not to feel sad that I've never had a kiss in real life.

It's not just anticipation of escape that makes my head full of buzzing insects all week. There's a lot of stress about Westminster, which is convenient as my tenseness is even less noticeable. I'm so close to getting out I can almost taste it.

I look at the gifts my stalker-ghost gave me and remind myself someone thought I was worth that risk, before returning the ring to the broken seam of my hoody.

The girl who was given a ring, a book, and kisses is capable of pulling off a bold escape. I've got my outfit ready for tomorrow: my hoody and my favourite jeans. Though I'm wearing my hoody to bed as usual since it's cool tonight. I'm all set to never see any of this life again.

There is one thing I'll miss. My ghost.

Whoever it is who is stalking me, leaving me gifts and messages, and I suspect, sometimes watching me in the garden. I can't be certain my stalker is a man, but sometimes

I catch a sweep of scent. A moment of ocean salt and fresh air.

Tomorrow.

Tomorrow I will enter the supermarket and walk straight back out to the taxi rank. From there, I've got the route mapped out to get to Scotland.

I'm nervous. Excited. I need to sleep, because tomorrow will be big.

4

FELICITY

A warm dry palm stifles my scream as the gunfire yanks me awake.

"Cara," a deep voice whispers in my ear. "All is well."

He's leaning over me, and though we've only met once, I know him.

Marco. The scent of salt and the outdoors, his voice, and his shadowed face are familiar. My wrists are pinned and my mind whirls as more shots are fired. There are yells and grunts.

Evidently all is *not* well.

I pull on my wrists, but he's holding me tight.

"We need to go now. Will you be a good girl and stay quiet for me?"

I fight. Kicking and wriggling, but not screaming. Whatever is going on, I won't draw attention to myself.

That's when the tang of ammunition reaches my nostrils. Acrid and smoky. It occurs to me that if he wanted me dead, I'd have never woken.

Doesn't mean I'm going to let him wreck all my plans. I

won't be another kingpin's captive. I bite at his hand, thrash, and try to claw at him. Just because he was kind to me once doesn't mean he will be again. This could be my chance to get out of my father's house. Unexpected, yes, but no less welcome for that.

A frustrated snarl comes from deep in Marco's chest as he uncovers my lips for an instant before his mouth lands on mine.

What?

Why is Marco...? My lips soften under the pressure and my mind goes blank. I forget about escaping him.

As first kisses go, this is...

There's the snick of plastic and a sharp pinch at my wrists, slamming them together. The covers are tugged away, leaving my legs bare.

It's not a kiss.

Marco is not kissing me. He's preventing me from screaming as he gathers my ankles together, his grip uncompromising and his mouth hard. Another zip tie, and I jackknife myself, trying to knee him. I try to scream now, but it's too late.

I'm caught.

He lifts me with surprising gentleness, one hand under my shoulders and the other on my bum, mouth still on mine, my arms trapped between us. Slipping out of my room he moves down the corridor in assured but silent strides.

I don't know what to do, whether to try to struggle or try to shout. Who is the biggest threat here? Brent, who is kidnapping me? The Westminster mafia, sending smoke and yells through the house? If I managed to get away from Brent and jumped two-footed through the house like the world's most malcoordinated kangaroo, would Westminster kill me? Would Kensington—given he didn't even give me his name—even think to search for me?

A sob tries to rise up out of my belly. Escape was so near.

I stop fighting. Brent is massive, and zip ties are impossible to break, so it would be futile. Besides, he seems intent on getting me out. He moves confidently through the maze of narrow corridors. At the bottom of the first flight of stairs, he pauses in a dark alcove as there's gunfire. Close, far too close.

"Okay?" he whispers against my lips.

"Let me go," I hiss.

"Don't be afraid." I feel his words as much as hear them. "I'm going to protect you."

I try to be angry. He's captured me against my will and I really should be furious. But honestly, the massive warm bulk of his body pressed to mine and his arms around me make this the most cared for I've felt in since my mother died. Which is a timely reminder of how this will end.

"You." I have to swallow before I can continue that sentence because my throat is dry as overcooked sponge cake. "Fucker."

He huffs with laughter and hitches me up his body. "Put your arms around my neck."

Slowly I obey, my body having a will of its own.

He hums approval.

It's as though my weight is nothing at all and despite the chaos around us, I'm not scared. I trust he's not going to allow anything to happen to me.

"You're doing so well," he says in the same low voice as the noise in the corridor beside us recedes.

He moves with sure, light steps to an old servants'

entrance. Pausing by the door, he squeezes me to him reassuringly as a black SUV pulls up.

I don't know how, but he opens the door still holding me and before I've really thought through the implications of leaving with him, I'm on the spacious back seat, and we're speeding away. I look back through the rear window, and there's a flickering yellow glow in the window of the second floor as well as the fading crack of gunfire.

"What was that about?" I snap, turning away from the place I grew up in.

"You were in danger," he replies calmly as he kneels before me. The back of this car is excessively spacious. "I wish you hadn't forced me to do this."

"Force you to abduct me?" I watch as he slices off the plastic zip tie from my ankles and rubs his thumb over the red place where my skin was constricted.

"The constraint. I hoped you'd come with me willingly, knowing you're safe with me." Marco moves to the seat and smooths his hands down my arms and over my hands. I consider kicking him as he releases my wrists, but it seems a churlish way to get myself tied up again, and I'd do better to wait for a chance to escape. And besides, him carrying me, restraining me, and kneeling at my feet has done something odd to my insides. Liquified them. I'm frozen soup, thawed and moulding to his heat.

It's only when he clasps my hands in his that I see I'm trembling. Shaking uncontrollably all over.

"Did he die?" I ask in a whisper. Shock, I guess.

"I think so, yes." Softly, like I'm a flighty woodland creature he's captured and trying to keep quiet. "Westminster were very angry when they found he couldn't repay his debt." Marco doesn't ask who I mean. My father might have been a sub-standard parent—the best things he gave were decent skin and strong impetus towards entrepreneurialism —but I probably should care he's dead. A true daughter, a loyal member of the mafia, would feel sad.

I don't. I feel nothing.

"And everyone else?" It's not that I liked all the mobsters, but... Gone?

"I'm sorry, cara."

The silence in the car is as thick as the noise and smoke we came from and my brain won't work properly, still fugged with sleep and disbelief. Despite everything that's happened, I can't stop sneaking looks at my... I'm going with kidnapper? But I have a question mark over other possible terms to swap in, some of which are less disturbing, some... Not.

Saviour. Mafia boss. Guardian angel. Abductor. Inappropriate older crush.

...Stalker?

Is stalker better or worse than kidnapper?

Ope. Who knows?

He's wearing dark trousers and a charcoal grey shirt unbuttoned at the neck and sleeves rolled to the elbow, revealing muscled forearms covered with black hair that makes me long to pet him.

I keep my hands to myself and run my thumb over the bulging seams of my hoody as I look at him from the corner of my eye, my nose a shadow over what I'm trying to see.

I don't know how long it is until we stop and Marco opens the door. I follow instinctively, but when I go to stand, he tuts and sweeps me into his arms, one hand at my knees and the other under my shoulder blades.

And oh god I shouldn't like this mode of transport so much. Forget bicycles or roller skates, Marco is the most fun way to get from A to B. I surreptitiously sniff his skin and it must be pure pheromone, because I don't know what he smells like except something that makes my insides quiver. The heat of him penetrates wherever we touch, and his hold on my bare legs is fire.

"Welcome to my home."

"I can walk," I protest as he strides across the gravel and in through a massive open door, spilling yellow light like a magic portal. Because this much enjoyment of being carried is not healthy.

"Without shoes?" he points out and, yeah. Maybe not. I shut up but there's a low hum and I wonder if my ears are ringing from the gunfire.

"Put me down," I insist as soon as we're through the door, blinking at the light.

Marco nods and rolls his eyes with fond wryness and the hubbub peters out slowly as he slips me down his body. For a second we're the only two people in the world. My hoody and top ruck up and the soft warmed cotton of his shirt brushes my stomach. I look into his light blue gaze and the hunger I saw in his face when we met is back, carnal and fierce. Low in my belly, something responds.

His hands are still holding me, stabilising me and I tip up my chin in invitation.

The hum brightens.

There's... Applause. I turn my head away from Marco's mesmerising gaze, and only then do I notice the rows of staff. Bulky mafia goons in suits, but also neatly dressed household staff all smiling, nudging each other, clapping and whooping. There are calls of, "Boss, finally!" and "Get in!".

I stare. Confounded.

It's the middle of the night and they've all but rolled out a red carpet and bunting.

In one of my favourite historical romances there's a scene where the aristocratic hero brings his bride home to his enormous country estate. The servants are all lined up in an intimidatingly formal parade. She charms them all, and wins the duke's heart as well.

This is like that scene, and yet. Not at all. There's no hostility when my glance darts over the faces in the crowd. They're not haughty. I don't have to win them over; they're predisposed to like me.

Is this what Marco gets every time he comes home after nefarious mafia business is concluded? I sneak a look at him and he's glaring at a man near the front with dirty blond hair, glasses, and an immaculate three-piece suit.

What's going on?

A middle-aged woman approaches with a tray of daintily iced mini cupcakes and a cup of tea and I stare, confused, at what seems to be my favourite herbal tea.

I've slipped into an alternative dimension. Only explanation. First the ghost. Now this.

It's a dream. I'm going to wake up with drool on my pillow and my phone screeching at me to bring coffee to my father's office, stat.

"Paulo, is everything as we discussed?" Marco says behind me.

The man with blond hair steps forward. "Stage two of operation why... Uh." He coughs. "Whisky has been implemented as best we could, sir."

Marco shoots a disparaging look at Paulo and puts his hand on the small of my back. I can't help but lean into his touch.

"What's Operation Whisky?"

"Some..." He sighs with exasperation. "Important logistics."

Oh. He does like whisky then. Huh. I assumed he didn't, and we had that in common. I'm irrationally sad.

"Tell me what would make you feel comfortable?"

I think about the unhinged things I could say, and I wonder if he'd do them. Things like, *stroke my hair, take me to bed and cuddle me, drape me over the table and make me yours.* I settle for something merely weird.

5

MARCO

Those pyjamas are going to kill me. Cherry-patterned pyjama shorts that reveal her long smooth legs.

It's been almost a month since we met, and Felicity has been in every one of my senses all that time. I can't forget her vanilla and berries scent, the vivid feel of her warm skin, the sound of her lyrical voice that has a thousand chords inside it, all harmonious.

Something in me awoke when I saw her, a possessive creature stirred and focused, and growled, *mine*. And finally that creature is content.

I love seeing her in my home. My girl, safe in my house, protected. And maybe so does she, because her answer to what will make her comfortable isn't going back to where she's lived her whole life, or being with her family.

She's suspicious, unused to being the centre of attention and seemingly not sure she likes it. But despite her fear and the fact it's the middle of the night, she gulps and whispers, "That tea, a cupcake, a book, and then to go to bed?"

I grab the tea tray from Maria, giving her a nod of approval. They're all going to get chastised for making such a big scene and Paulo might be laughing now, but he nearly made it sound like I'd plotted this whole incident to catch my girl. Which is only partially true. I was still working out the details of my seduction when the situation with Westminster happened. I'm not one to turn away opportunities.

"Come," I say to Felicity. "All of you lot are dismissed," I toss over my shoulder. They've worked hard to ensure everything is perfect for Felicity, and I'm grateful. But right now I need my girl to myself. It's only a minute to make our way across the house, and Felicity's mouth drops as I swing the library door open. She makes a gurgling noise.

"Are you alright?"

"Yes," she squeaks. "I just... Wow."

I suppose it is quite impressive.

Two floors high, the pale wood gleams. There are multiple ladders on wheels, and discreet labels separate sections on virtually every topic and genre. All the knowledge you might need, and the entertainment. My collection of murder mystery novels takes up floor to ceiling for twenty feet. But I don't think that's what she was thinking of when she said a book.

"I think this nook will particularly interest you."

I lead her to an area by the window with a big plush squashy chair, a plate of cupcakes on the small table, and bookshelves surrounding at almost arm's length.

She regards the shelves suspiciously.

"Do you think there's something you'll want to read?" I ask innocently. I'm not going to confess I picked up on her book downloads while I was investigating her father's financial situation. Or building this corner of my library especially for her. To make her happy.

"Yeah. I like these authors." She gestures at the rows of books.

It doesn't even occur to her to ask why something is as she likes it. I know without asking it's not because she expects it—her eyes are like saucers. No, it's because she thinks it's a coincidence. The concept that someone has gone to effort for her is as alien as the smutty sci-fi romances she reads. She doesn't ask because she assumes this is for someone else.

In time she'll understand that nothing is too much trouble. That she can ask for anything she wants and I'll just tell her that the outrageously expensive requests will be delivered immediately but the impossible will take a little longer.

"You can read whatever you want from here. Just take it."

She screws up her face in scepticism. "Whatever I like?"

"Yes."

"You'll check up on what I'm reading," she scoffs. "Limit the number of books."

I shrug. "How many books were you thinking of taking?"

"Book collecting and reading are separate hobbies," she says defensively.

"You think I am not aware of that?" I raise one eyebrow and glance at my library. "I have read many of these books, but of course there are more I haven't even opened."

She bites her lip as she regards the thousands of volumes that surround us.

Picking a few books from the shelf, she starts reading the backs.

I'm reminded of how she chose the books at the supermarket. So serious and analytical, as though this one decision would determine her future, rather than merely a few hours of enjoyment. A moment later she sinks into the padded seat to assess the books she short-listed.

I purr inwardly at the sight. Almost exactly as I imagined her when I arranged this part of the library myself. Except that ideally I'd be behind her and she'd lean back and snuggle into me.

She catches me looking and bolts upright. "I wasn't—"

"It's okay." I approach slow and cautious, as though I were touching a wild animal, I place my hand on her sternum and push her backwards. The cotton of the hoody touches my fingertips, but it's the heat under my palm that sends blood rushing to my cock. She lets out a soft whimper and squirms, her lips parting as I press her into the seat. "Relax. Take all the time you need."

At my command, she does, eyes still darting around, unable to settle fully. But suppressing that urge to run, so reluctantly I lift my hand.

She blinks, nods, and sorts through the books again, re-reading the cover of one with a woman in a long blue dress.

I sink into the window seat and watch her. So pretty. Her coffee-with-a-drop-of-milk-coloured hair that will be wrapped around my fist as I tug her head back one day soon. Her pink lips, perfect for sliding over the head of my cock. I've never wanted anyone like I do Felicity. But it's been a lot for her tonight, without being lusted after by a man almost twice her age. I can play a longer game.

"Can I borrow this one," she asks eventually, holding up the one with a woman in a red dress.

I nod and she almost smiles in response.

"I'll show you to your bedroom."

I see the moment she notices the open window behind me. A crack to vent in the air. It's a split second of her focus, so swift that if I wasn't as attuned to her as I am, I'd have missed it. Smart, my girl. Used to concealment, she doesn't show that she saw the potential escape route.

"Just one thing, cara," I say as we're climbing the stairs. "Don't try my patience by attempting to escape." My voice goes hard without my volition. I won't allow her to put herself in danger.

This isn't the way I hoped we'd meet again. I wanted to get her out from her father's clutches and woo her gently, as she deserves.

But I saved her, I kidnapped her, and while if she really wishes to leave, I'll provide everything to make her life comfortable, I'd rather she stayed. It's not unreasonable to want the chance to win her over and bring her happily to my bed and have her as my bride.

Her mouth flattens. "I'm a prisoner here. Nothing has changed."

"You're my guest." Until she's my wife, that is.

"But I can't leave." Fingering the cuffs of her hoody, she glares at me, eyes and voice like steel.

"It's the middle of the night. We'll talk about tomorrow in the morning." That would be my preference, anyway, but I suspect my stubborn girl has other ideas. I'll be ready. "You're not leaving."

6

FELICITY

There was an open window in the library.

I lie in the massive, very comfortable bed and think about my life turned inside out and upside down, and the potential of that open window.

My father is dead. That means he won't come looking for me. I'm safe from his influence and if I get away, I'd have a real chance of escape. I have with me almost all the things I'd have run away with—except more sensible clothes.

Part of me wants to wait until the morning. Marco saved me, and where my father has fear and brutality, he has loyalty. It's obvious his people respect him in a way no one at the Kensington mafia ever did my father. Maybe whatever he has planned wouldn't be so bad?

We'll talk about tomorrow in the morning.

I've been fobbed off.

Do you think this was what it was like for my mother at first? Maybe my father was charming and kind before he got bored of her. Perhaps he even promised marriage, and my mother thought he would eventually make an honest woman of her. He probably didn't start off with, *You'll be nothing to me and your daughter will be my servant.*

Marco isn't like that. He wants to take care of you, a voice whispers in my head.

Sure, his attention gave me the confidence to finally decide to enact my escape plan, but that doesn't mean he's not dangerous. He is still a deadly mafia kingpin.

And there's that other voice.

You don't deserve a man like him. You won't be able to keep the interest of a gorgeous, powerful, wealthy kingpin for long. He'll get bored of you.

I want to believe the affection in Marco's eyes, the feeling of rightness when I was held in his arms. The inclination of my heart to trust him, fall asleep, and enjoy his attention for as long as I have it. But I don't want my heart broken when he inevitably decides I'm not enough, as everyone else thinks.

Perhaps he doesn't want you at all. Maybe you're a mafia bargaining chip.

There's no way I'm staying as his little hostage.

I crawl out of bed before I can change my mind. I'll get out, run to a road. It didn't work when I tried it from my father's house, but he's gone.

I silently try the door handle. Unlocked.

The night air is cool, and there's moonlight spilling silver onto the long passageway. I noted the route down to the library. All I have to do is not get caught.

I take a shaky breath and one step forward. I can do this.

No klaxon sounds. No trap goes off. Another, and another, on silent feet.

At the end of the corridor, I hear his deep voice. "Felicity."

Oh god. The kingpin.

I turn, my body already trembling. He stands outside a now-open door opposite the one I came from, partially hidden by shadows. He's shirtless. I can make out only the outline of his physique from this distance and in the white moonlight, since he's half hidden by the shadows. But I can see muscles and a crisscross of scars.

"I told you, we'll discuss this in the morning. I'll take you wherever you want to go. Provide whatever you want. Be it cakes or books or freedom."

He seems sincere, and yet I take a tentative step backwards. The kingpin is huge. Muscled. Strong, yes, but I bet he's not fast. And I have a massive advantage. He'll assume I'm going for the front door and there's easily enough space for me to turn back to the library on noiseless bare feet.

I'm good at being quiet and quick. Lots of practice.

"Go back to bed, cara." The command reverberates through me.

I nearly do it. There's a battle of wills going on up and down forty feet of corridor shrouded in darkness.

That rough tone. The stark beauty of his unclothed but scarred body. I'm a bit scared, yes, but there's also another emotion bubbling up.

I'm excited. I shake my head.

"That's the game you want to play, is it?" he purrs.

I take another step away. I think I can make it to the window. I *must*. Because while adrenaline is pulsing in my blood, right from my heart to every extremity, and throbbing at my core, I can't lose.

"Try then. But if I catch you, you'll be mine."

His.

I run.

I've taken off before I can think through the consequences. His heavy thudding strides follow. Exhilaration races through me. Running, my legs and arms moving, alive after so many years of stasis.

He was offering something normal, to talk about the future in the morning. But I couldn't settle and now all his attention is on me as I try to escape. I screech around the corner of the corridor and throw myself into the open hallway, the smooth white walls and occasional minimalist painting reflecting moonlight.

My muscles burn with the effort of running.

And oh does it feel good. I check over my shoulder and his eyes are trained on me, intent as a predator. He's focused. I whip my head back around. He's chasing after me like he wants me, like that kiss meant something and he won't let me go.

I should be tired after waking in the middle of the night, but I'm more energised than I've been in my life as I sprint down across and take the stairs two at a time. I can hear him behind me, but not close enough to see, I'm pretty sure.

That's not disappointment. It's not.

I'm getting out of here.

I round the corner at the bottom of the stairs and slow, trying to control my breathing, which is fast and from the whole of my lungs, my chest heaving, throat on fire. But I make my bouncing steps light on the cold marble flooring.

The sound of him coming after me doesn't pause. I grin. I've outfoxed him. I glance back, confident that—

He's there. Right behind me. I shriek with fright and accelerate. I'm really sprinting now.

Half of my heart wants to escape. It's beating oxygenated blood around my limbs and urging me faster and onwards. It's reminding me why I was trying to leave the mafia life in the first place. That part of me is trying to get away and has real panic at the thought of being caught.

But the other half... Oh, the other half wants to run too. But that section of my heart is gleeful. Looking for places to slow or trip. Urging me to look behind again and check he's following, and see the intent look on his face. This part of my heart delights that he wants me so much. Enough that he'll chase me through his house in the dead of night.

This part of my heart *wants to be caught.*

His promise. I'll be *his*. That ought to be terrifying, by all rights, but it's not. I need to own and be owned. I crave the intensity and the struggle, the proof that he'll overcome my every objection, even as my feet slap painfully on the floor.

To be owned by him wouldn't be slavery as it was with my father. No, his mafia loves him as their leader, that is clear. If I were owned by him, I'd be an indulged pet, given every best titbit and snuggled. Protected.

It couldn't last. I know that, and I want freedom more, even if I'll be alone again. Scotland is the only option.

I can hear him and my fogged brain thinks I can smell his sweat and feel his heat. He's a force of nature.

My lungs are close to bursting with the unfamiliar effort of running and I'm heaving in air, panting with my whole chest. My knees hurt with the force juddering up through them with every stride, cracking up my bones. Every muscle in my body is engaged.

There. I recognise the entrance to the library at the end of the corridor and my mind, seeing freedom is possible, pushes my legs faster. I half expect him to pounce as I throw the door open in front of me like the melodramatic arrival of a queen, but no. He's at my heels though, his hard breathing close.

This is one of those moments in a film where the plucky heroine gets out, despite insurmountable odds. There's an epic soundtrack that's swelling to a crescendo. I'm going to dive through that window like Indiana Jones rolling out of a doomed temple.

The wooden floor is shiny and as I round the corner to my reading nook, I almost lose my footing, sliding to the side. Only Marco's arm as he reaches out saves me from crashing into the bookshelf, but I manage to evade being grasped, and then—

The window is closed.

The two halves of my heart squeeze together.

I lunge for it anyway, across the big window seat, expecting to feel Marco's big body smash into me as I yank the handle and fall onto the cushions. It doesn't budge. Locked.

Of course it is.

Marco doesn't land on top of me as I expect, and my heart stutters. He doesn't need to.

I'm caught.

I turn slowly, creeping onto my knees and stare at his bare chest. He's standing at the edge of the window seat. Suddenly I could throw up, I'm so sick with regret. I'll deserve this punishment. I'll take it bravely, I promise myself.

I shouldn't have run. Stupid.

"Look at me." His voice is implacable. This isn't a request.

Miserably, I raise my eyes at a snail's pace. What revenge will he take? I can't cope with any more pain. I curl into myself even as I'm compelled to look at his face. An angry mob boss is a terrifying creature.

I hesitate at his neck. I don't want to find anger where there used to be affection.

But when I meet his gaze, in his face isn't fury or disappointment. Just understanding and patience. Possessiveness and... love?

All my fears melt away like ice in a hot drink.

"Say no, cara," he states. "Say no, clear and loud, if you don't want to be *mine*."

I open my mouth but sound doesn't come out. I even form the word, but my tongue sticks to the top of my mouth.

He won, fair and square. He promised not to harm me. He gave reasonable demands—for a mafioso.

I accepted the risk when I ran, so although he's telling me I could refuse, I don't. I swallow, and his gaze flicks down to my neck.

He nods, taking my silence for acceptance, which it honestly is, and sinks down onto the cushions of the window seat.

"So beautiful. I'm going to spoil you," he murmurs as he pulls me into his lap and leans back into the cushions. Too confused to struggle, I let myself rest on him and he hums with contentment. While I'm still breathing heavily, my chest tight, he's utterly calm.

That wasn't even a competition. He could have snatched me up at any point, I realise, but he let me come down to see for myself that he'd already thought to bar my exit.

"Why did you run from me?" His hands are clamps on my side and back and when I peek up his stare is uncompromising but somehow kind.

Why did I run? Because of my whole life. This isn't one or two sentences, but I suppose it boils down to this. "I was scared. Why did you chase me?"

"You'd have hurt your feet on the gravel. Why were you scared?"

Because I didn't plan for this to happen, and I don't

know what to make of this connection between us. But I don't think he'll accept that, because that wasn't the cause of the fear. Not really. And the relentlessness of his hold and the quiet patience as he waits informs me he's not going to be satisfied until I've confessed all.

So I do. It pours out of me.

All that has happened. My mother. My father. The things I've seen. Why I want to go to Scotland. He listens and strokes my back, with a thunderous rumble when I tell him something particularly unpleasant. He demands that I show him each scar, and I try to remember which one is which. He strokes his palm over the old hurts. It shouldn't do anything, but it does, wiping away the residual, lingering pain. Those stories are mostly associated with the escape plans that didn't work, and his eyes are glacial. But when I tell him about the one that nearly did, oh, that's different. There's a gleam in his summer-sky eyes then, and when I press my cheek to his stubbled one, I can feel his smile.

He nods and chuckles and murmurs, "I knew it. So clever," as I explain how I stole from my father and was going to get away. He wants to know every detail, and I swear it sounds like he's proud of me. The low purr of approval from his chest relaxes me more than any tea, cake, or novel I've experienced.

I find myself soaking up his warm strength and breathing in his scent. Not the ocean, exactly. It's been a long day. Night. Whatever.

He smells like sweat on a warm summer breeze, fresh air and musk and... something male. When I slump down, his chest is warm and solid, even as his chest hair tickles my nose and is the tiniest bit abrasive.

We lapse into silence and I start to look at my captor in the moonlight. Every part of him is gorgeous and different to what I feel on my own body. Where I'm slight and podgy, he's firm and muscled. And those scars. His chest and arms are covered with marks that indicate the brutal life he's led. And yet he's holding me with so much tender care. He's strong.

Need rises like a cake cooking low in my belly.

He chased me. Snippets come back. The pounding of my heart and our feet. The flare of excitement and the thrill. The inevitability of him catching me.

He still hasn't taken anything and the fuzzy-edged images of what he might want from me pucker my nipples under my camisole even as they sharpen in my mind's eye. The details get clearer. His hand in my hair, urging my mouth onto his cock as I watch his light blue eyes darken with lust. A flash of his dark stubble as I turn to see him as he takes me from behind on my hands and knees.

I want that.

"All your planning. It seems a pity to lose it entirely. Anticlimactic. You want to go to Scotland in the morning?" he asks eventually.

I hesitate. Surely I do. I don't want to be his, like he said. I don't want to be owned and petted and coddled. I'll be okay up in cold Scotland, on my own. "Yes."

"Okay."

Nodding is harder than it should be. It feels like this is the end of our conversation, but I can't let it finish.

"I thought..." Did he not mean it? About me being his?

"What is it?" He presses a kiss on the top of my head.

I roll words around my brain like marbles.

"I thought you'd..." I thought he'd hold me down and take my virginity, that's what I thought. "Do whatever you wanted to me. Because you said I'm yours." Just that idea makes heat bloom again between my legs and I wriggle in his lap, pressing my thighs together.

This doesn't mean I trust him. How can I? I know how these mafia bosses work. It's not real without a marriage. He'll tire of me. I'm very tiresome.

But in the meantime, maybe I can allow myself to give in, and he'll make me feel good.

"Exactly," he says, low and rough. "I cherish what's mine. I wouldn't hurt you or force you. When I slip into your tight pussy you'll be soaking wet and begging me."

Oh…

Oh my. Yes, I'm really not far from begging.

"You want that possession. To be owned." It's not a question. He's seen inside me and knows.

A delicious shiver goes down my back. I hide my face in his chest as I nod. Yes. I want the comfort of decisions made for me, to be looked after and cosseted. It's been so long that I've been alone with every burden.

"Have I disappointed you?"

My throat seizes up. "Maybe."

"Well," he murmurs. "We can't have that now, can we?"

7

MARCO

She's all soft curves and nervous sexual energy in my arms. So fucking sweet and a temptation like no other. So enticing.

Every part of me thrums with the desire to roll her underneath me, push that tease of fabric aside and thrust into her.

"You've been so brave and strong." Everything that has happened to her makes my heart ache. "But you don't have to be, anymore. Lie back, and let me take care of you."

Now she's with me, and I'm going to please her. That's my whole reason for living.

Those dove grey eyes blink uncertainly as I lift her from my lap and lay her back onto the cushions, dragging extras to go beneath her head so she's at just the right angle to watch me eat her pussy, and under her hips to give me all the access I want.

I take my time kissing down her body, pulling her old hoody up to access her skin. The dip between her breasts is still covered in that little camisole with a frilly edge and a bow. She clutches my hair as I slip the neckline down and reveal one plush breast, then further, and I admire her dusky pink nipple before I devour it.

She writhes, unable to figure out if she's seeking more or evading it, overcome. Her fingers tighten on my hair.

"You like that don't you, my sensitive girl. So responsive to me."

"Uhh." Her reply is just a moan of desire as I reveal her other breast and bite gently on it. I could tease her like this forever, and one day I'll dedicate hours to worshipping this perfect chest. But right now I want to see her luscious pussy.

The innocent cuteness of her flat stomach and belly button leads to the waistband of those damn shorts. I slide it down, and *yes*. No underwear. I groan and take a moment to palm my cock through my boxers.

During our chase I thought I could see peeks of her sweet, rounded butt cheeks as she ran, revealed by her shorts riding up. And I was right. "Your curves are mouth-watering, you know that?"

"No?"

I huff a laugh into her cotton-covered abdomen. "You are. You're my perfect girl."

I keep one hand cupping her hip, holding her to me and urging her closer. The other I trail down her stomach, smiling to myself as she squeaks and tries to withdraw from my touch.

Nope. Not happening.

And I must be losing my mind, because instead of removing her shorts, I keep them on, teasing us both by kissing her through the fabric, getting lower and lower. Her legs are already spread to accommodate my kneeling between them but it takes no more than a tiny nudge and she opens further for me. Over her mons I brush my fingertips, further down, until I feel what I'm searching for. The loose fabric gapes and reveals one side of her pussy, glistening.

"Such a lovely welcome," I say, and my voice is gravelly with arousal. I push the fabric aside—damp. The sign that makes my cock even harder in my boxers. Her pink folds shift as she tries to get contact on her clit, and she whimpers softly with need.

"That's it," I say and let my mouth touch her and she lets out a moan like relief and frustration balled into one.

Yes. That wetness, not from my mouth. This is seeping out of her, just for me. I take one long lick at her seam, a greedy taste of her honey.

"Good girl being so wet for me." I get my lips onto her then, a simple press of a kiss, but she chokes and her legs scrabble for purchase.

Ha. I can provide that. I clamp my palms over both of her ankles and this time I go right to her clit and suck.

She keens, so hot and wound up. Desperate to come.

It's a promise, this act tonight. I'll give her everything she needs if she'll trust me. No more running away.

I reward her for being mine alone. I gorge. I get my whole mouth and cheeks in that beautiful pussy of hers, covering myself in her juices as I suck and lick at her. I thrust my tongue into her tight passage for the joy of her taste. I lap at her hard, using the flat of my tongue, and she chases me when I try different patterns and rhythms to find what makes her tear apart

"You're so delicious." I love that she's made herself crazy for this, and all I have to do is set her off. She's my firework, but I'm certain, having watched her for weeks, that she's like this for me alone. When anyone else touched her she shied away. There was no melting like she is now.

I'm going to make it so sweet and hot and all she deserves. She's mine to care for, and to breed, though I haven't said that second bit yet. I don't want to scare my girl away with my obsession. But it's going to happen. I'll be inside her, filling her up with my come. Painting her with the seed that will make her lush and ripe. Fuck, I cannot wait to see my girl pregnant with our child.

While I like pinning her ankles down, there's a more important thing I want to feel. I release her and place one forearm banded over her lower belly to keep her in place, and bring my other hand to that little hole. A touch and she cries out. I slide in one finger right up to the second joint and she is so slick it goes in easily. She arches—good thing I have her held by the hips. So then it's a second finger—tight, so tight now—and I fuck her with them. I curl up to rub that sensitive spot inside her, and suck her clit. I'm covered in her and revelling in the sweet and salt taste of her, the yielding pink flesh of her soaked pussy as my fingers stroke into her harder and faster. I'll never get enough.

Her hands find my head and comb through my hair then grip. A tightening of pain, and I relish it for how possessive she's being. This isn't one-sided, of me giving her an orgasm with my tongue. With her hands on me, holding me to her, she's claiming me as surely as I am her. She's taking ownership of this otherwise dubious situation, and the bite of her fingers on my scalp sends a message right down to my cock, making it throb. I want to be hers.

She's losing control, pulling me down in her search for the pleasure that will push her over the edge. I'm suffocating, drowning in her, and it's the most perfect way to die. So damn happy.

It doesn't take long like this, my fingers in her sweet wet passage, my tongue insistent, and her hands gripping me.

She clamps down on my fingers and screams. She's loud, my girl, and I can hardly repress a smugly satisfied grin as she jerks and cries, coming so hard she kicks me in the side repeatedly, hands tugging at my hair.

I don't let up. I ease her through it, feeling for when she needs more, harder to push her higher, then gradually backing off until she's collapsed, panting, and I'm softly kissing her inner thighs.

As I stretch out my cramped shoulders, fingers, and jaw, I take a moment to enjoy the sight of her. Ruined. Her eyes are shut, her cheeks are pink, and her dark hair is askew and haphazard over the cushions from where she's thrashed as she came. Her little cherry-patterned shorts are stretched out of shape and the hoody is still rucked up, revealing the swell of one breast. Her lashes are starred with tiny droplets of tears.

I lie down beside her and gather her into my arms. She comes willingly, soft and pliable as she accepts she's caught.

"You okay?" I ask, and pray I don't regret the question.

There's a shift of her skin on mine as she nods, then takes an inhale. Stops. Again. Taking a breath as though to begin talking, but doesn't.

"What is it?"

She hides her face against my chest, her soft cheek pressed to my pectoral and speaks into my skin. "Was that using me?"

"Oh, cara." She has no idea. "*Yes*. And I'll use you in other ways too, don't worry."

She lets out a shuddering sigh of what sounds like relief.

"I'm looking forward to using your beautiful body in filthy and depraved ways that make you cry for more."

"Really?" And there's uncertainty in the question I don't fully understand.

I stroke down the silk of her hair, reassuring. "I'll also treasure you."

Now I've had her tucked into me like this. Now I've made her come, the hunger isn't diminished. The sharp edge is off, but now my desire for her is deeper, wider. It's the ocean flooding up a brackish estuary. I thought I was obsessed before, but it's worse now. I love her.

She's told me what she wants: to go to Scotland, as far away from here—and me—as possible. And while I'll make that first part happen for her, there's no way it will involve me letting go.

I hold her closer to me and press my fingers into her waist. I breathe in her sweet strawberry and vanilla scent.

"You're *mine* now. Mine to give orgasms to." She sighs and rubs the corner of her mouth to my skin, the hair shifting beneath her lips. "Mine to care for. Mine to adore."

8

FELICITY

We lie together for a long time in the library. His big solid chest reassuringly my pillow and his arm my safety belt. I don't know whether I slept there, or what time it was when Marco slid my hoody back down, carried me upstairs and laid me into his bed. I was too exhausted and sated to think. But I remember his presence and rumbling voice telling me, "Go to sleep. It's been a long night."

I've never slept in the same bed as anyone. He's warm. Big, too. I hadn't thought of sleeping by myself as lonely. I'd just accepted it was cold, and tucked myself into a ball most nights and waited to fall asleep.

Being his means that he tucks me into his bed and spoons his body to my back. Slipping into oblivion with Marco at my back... That's different. For the first time in my life I'm not alone when I lose consciousness.

I wake to the scent of Marco on the pillow, salty ocean and musk, but no warm presence behind me. Cracking one eye open, I regard his bedroom with trepidation. It's austere and simple, only softened by the yellow light of dappled sunshine. Huge floor-to-ceiling windows open onto a woodland and I watch as a red and white and black bird swoops in and lands on a tree trunk.

He lives in the countryside, or has a garden so big it might as well be the countryside.

A bird feeder is hung high in the branches of a tree just outside the window, close. It's covered with half a dozen little birds of all colours, pecking away. They dive and squabble, their wings a blur. The birds with gold, red, and black markings stay on the feeder, jostling and feasting. But the little pink, white, and grey birds hang back, waiting for a gap then darting in to snatch a bit of food before beating their wings to fly away.

They all have their strategies, and have come to get their breakfast, confident in their provider.

Huh. Big scary mob boss likes to watch the birds.

And kidnap girls, give them orgasms, tell them they're his, make them think they've lucked out, then leave them alone. Why didn't he just allow me to escape?

"You're awake."

I scramble to roll over, clutching the covers to my chest even as relief floods into me. Marco is sitting in a blue armchair wearing a crisp white shirt open at the neck, revealing a strong, tanned neck and the dip between his collarbones. He has a laptop on his knees and is wearing black-rimmed reading glasses. And his mouth—the same mouth that he put on my pussy last night until I screamed with pleasure—turns up in a slow smile. It starts in his eyes and spreads across his face in a slide of light and heat like the sun rising on a summer's morning.

He removes his glasses and although I have a pang for the loss of his casual hot professor look, the better view of his pale blue eyes makes up for it. He appears happy to see me, and it makes me shy. I don't know what to do with this approval. I'm not used to it, and am half expecting to be told off for sleeping in, but he nods to his side of the bed.

"There's breakfast for you."

I turn and find a neat wooden tray covered with dozens of mini pastries, a cafetière of coffee, orange juice, a bowl of melon and strawberries, and what looks like blueberry muffins. My stomach rumbles in response and Marco's laughter washes over me, warm and affectionate as I blush.

"All my favourites," I mutter into a croissant, snatching it up before it's taken away.

"Always."

It's not a question about whether he stalked me, or an answer. But it skirts too close for me. What if it wasn't him? The crispy-soft buttery pastry in my mouth means I don't have to reply.

I think I'm almost willing to admit—to myself at least—I like that he watched me. If it was him. And sure, not having to tell him what I want to eat for breakfast is a bonus, but it's not the main reason. The truth is, the thought he's gone to trouble for me is the smell of perfectly-baked cupcakes: mouth-watering anticipation of comfort and delight.

What would it be like to bite into that proffered cupcake? To accept the promise of what he offered rather than going to Scotland?

True, he gave me up very easily, offering to send me north in the morning after he chased me last night. Will he still do that? The croissant suddenly feels dry in my mouth. I take a sip of orange juice, and despite it being fresh and sweet, all I can taste is the sour.

"When am I leaving?" This is like a band aid. Easier to cope with if I rip it off and make it hurt all at once.

Marco puts aside his laptop and comes over to the bed, towering over me. His height and the evident strength of his body makes my tummy squirm and my nipples stand to attention. He's gorgeous and I'm entirely in his power.

"Whenever you like," he says eventually. "You're not a prisoner."

I gulp. "Now."

Marco's lips tighten, but he doesn't comment. Just gestures for me to go with him, holding out his hand. His palm envelops mine with strong warmth.

I manage to not cry as I leave behind that delicious breakfast and sunlit bedroom where Marco slept with me, his arm possessively over my waist.

I should have said tomorrow, or never, because I'm desperate for more information about my captor. Trying to take in all the details of his home is futile. I crane my neck as I follow him downstairs, admiring abstract art and elegant sculptures in the modern but warm house. I'm still wearing my cotton pyjamas and hoody as we enter the marble-floored entrance hall and I wrap one arm uselessly around my ribcage.

A murmured request to a man waiting for Marco's command and a black limo purrs outside.

My heart is breaking. I don't want to do this. He's really going to let me go? After all his declarations last night. This morning. Whenever.

He leans over and brushes a kiss on my hair. "It's okay."

It's not. I have this feeling like I missed out the baking powder in my cake mixture. I've missed something important and it's all flat.

"I'm here," he murmurs. "Though my fingers might not be for much longer unless you stop trying to break them."

"What?" It's only when he lifts our joined hands that I realise I'm gripping onto him like he's the only thing holding me onto the planet. "Sorry," I mutter, tears prickling as I begin to withdraw my hand.

He doesn't let me, lacing our fingers together and squeezing.

"Come on." With his other arm, he holds me to his chest and carries me out to the limo, our hands still linked together. I don't want to let go.

He ducks into the limo and sets me down on the leather seat.

I have what I was aiming for. My savings, my father gone and not able to hunt me down. Freedom.

I need *him*. The kingpin who saw me, saved me, caught me, and has cared for me.

"Marco..."

He sits next to me and my heart pulses.

"What?" he asks casually, pulling me into his body. "You didn't think I was letting you go alone, did you?"

Yes. Idiot that I am, I thought he was sending me to Scotland, not accompanying me. Thank god. I have longer with Marco before the consequences of my poor, if seemingly rational, decisions materialise.

"How long does it take to get to Scotland?" I ask because I am apparently all in for torturing myself.

He shrugs one shoulder. "Six hours. Ish. But we need to make a couple of stops on the way."

Stops? What for?

9

MARCO

Apparently the mysterious and deadly reputation only works outside of my inner circle, as my second-in-command never ceases to give me shit. But he does get the job done. With no more than my vague order to Paulo as we left, we draw up outside a perfect little independent boutique.

"Are we going shopping?" my girl asks, confused, as I open the door and scoop her into my arms.

"Yep. You need something to wear that isn't those pyjamas. I might not get you any shoes though, so I have an excuse to carry you everywhere," I tease her.

"Marco, stop," she says urgently, eyes darting to and fro.

"What?" I don't stop. I shoulder our way in.

She wriggles and hisses, "I can't, we have to leave!"

The shop assistant, clearly well briefed by Paulo, flips the lock behind us, lowers the blinds, and slips into the backroom.

"You don't like the clothes?" I set her onto her feet and she snarls up at me like an angry kitten. I was so sure this would be her style. Sort of, relaxed-beach-girl vibe.

"I like them," she says, massaging her forehead, looking

at the floor, where her toes are curling. "But I haven't got any money to pay. I can't afford—"

"That's not an issue. I'm treating you."

"I'd be in your debt," she hugs herself with her arms and I manage not to step forwards and force her not to cover her beautiful body.

"The reverse. I am in *your* debt. I stole you from your home. You let me taste you last night." She begins to object to that phrasing, but I'm not listening to any nonsense. "You've trusted me. I'm merely requesting you allow me to give you some clothes since you haven't got any, and I feel responsible."

"I'd be doing you a favour, would I?" she asks with narrowed eyes and a sceptical furrow of her brow. She's unfurled a bit since she woke, but not enough.

"Yes, that's exactly it." I try to look innocent. Though honestly, she would be helping me out. If I see her much longer in that top that hints at the swell of her perfect tits and those tiny shorts, her long colt-like legs on display, I can't be held responsible for what I might do.

"Well, maybe just a pair of shorts and a top, so I have something other than these." She plucks at the cherry-pattern fabric, looking around with longing eyes. A bad habit. She's limiting this, fearful I'll pick through her expenditure like her father did.

"You need more than one outfit. I don't know if we'll be able to get anything from Kensington. Let's start with a hundred outfits."

"Don't be ridiculous," she scoffs, "I only need one."

There's some further negotiation about how many clothes I'll buy her, during which I manage to haggle her up to ten outfits, and settle into a comfortable sofa and watch as she browses. It's like when she was in the supermarket. She loves pretty things, but I can see her checking the tags and assessing the price and the value.

The first thing she tries on is a deep indigo colour skimpy silk top with a lace trim, and a pair of cut-off jean shorts. I almost groan. It's basically as revealing as those fucking pyjamas. Yes, it's summer, but could she not choose something that wasn't torture? She's going to kill me.

She fingers the silk and turns to look from all angles in the mirror.

"It's so nice," she whispers. "Can I have it?"

"Yes," I answer without hesitation. Even if it probably will be the cause of my demise. There was me thinking it would be one of the other mafias, but nope. Felicity in that top and those shorts will do it.

"I didn't even say please," she objects, blinking in disbelief.

"Even better. What else are you going to demand?"

"What about..." She points at a rack of hoodies. Unlike the camisole, there's nothing sexy about them. Just cute. Maybe she thinks that she's only allowed sexy clothes?

"You can have that too."

"I didn't even say which one, or how much they cost," she huffs. "How can you be sure?"

"Because, one, anything will look great on you. And two, I don't care about the cost. I can afford it."

It's difficult for her. She's been told she doesn't deserve anything, and however hard she has fought, shit like that sticks.

"Believe me, you would have to work much harder than this to put a dent in my finances. You can buy the whole shop and every other shop on the street and it wouldn't be even a small percentage. But even if it were, I'd still do this."

"But why?" There's bafflement in her voice and she

scuffs her bare feet on the floorboards, her dark hair falling over her face.

I tilt my head and consider. There are a thousand reasons, and it's just a matter of which she wants to hear right now. *Because I love you* is the simplest, but not for this moment.

When I don't answer immediately she peeks from under that protective waterfall, her grey eyes pale with expectation of being rejected.

"You deserve it."

She splutters with disbelieving laughter. "What?"

"For being strong and brave and you," I say matter-of-factly. "For being the one I want, and for being mine."

Her eyes light and there's a second of her smile before she covers her mouth with her hands. So happy over some clothes. Spoiling her will be a joy.

She pads over to a rack of dresses. Floor length, black with a bold flower pattern, strapless, with a long split up one side that reveals her leg. She glances at me as she strips off right there, in the main part of the shop, and slips the dress over her head. The confidence of the gesture is that of a sultry girl and it suits her.

"What about this one?"

"Of course."

Approaching me with slow, deliberate, steps she widens her eyes, slides her finger over her inner bottom lip and drags it across. Coy and sexy and knowing and pure.

"Please Mr scary mafioso, please can I have the expensive dress?" I lean back and my hard-on tents my trousers. I don't bother to hide it. I think she'll like to see the effect she has on me. Nothing like a man being helpless with desire to make a woman feel powerful.

"Please? I really like it." She makes puppy eyes at me.

I'm nonplussed for a second, then get it. She's never asked for what she wanted before. She's too proud to beg, because pleading never made any difference with her father. But this is a strange sort of truth. She's asking, but she knows I'll say yes. She's realised this shopping trip can be a fun game she can play safely with me.

I put on a severe expression. "Will you wear it? It's not okay to waste clothes."

"I promise I'll wear it." She does a little twirl, showing off the dress, but I only have eyes for the girl inside.

"But only for me," I say sternly. "It's very revealing. I won't have any other man looking at you."

"Why not?" She blinks up at me, all naivety.

"Because I'd have to kill them, cara," I say, then sigh with mock regret. "I currently have a good reputation as a fair but demanding boss. If you show other men—even my men—that gorgeous body of yours, you'll make me a wild animal." I palm my hand over the solid length of my cock and she follows the movement. That regard turns the slight pressure into a stream of sparks. "You'll be a siren, luring men to their deaths."

She snorts with laughter but when she sees my face remain serious a shiver goes through her...

"Does that mean I can have it?" She tips her chin down and looks from under lowered lashes.

I sigh thoughtfully, take my reading glasses from my pocket and beckon her to me with one hand. There's an extra sway in her hips as she approaches and I go to slip my glasses on. "Let me have a look at this dress you want so much, mmm?"

"I think this is a good angle." She drops to her knees between my thighs.

My reading glasses drop, forgotten.

Probably a good man would refuse with some shit about how he doesn't want her feeling that she owes me this for some clothes. But fuck, I'm not a good man. Never pretended to be. My belt buckle clinks as she undoes it, clumsy in her inexperience with men's clothing, and my cock presses up. Eager. So fucking desperate for her touch.

"Go on," I growl when she pauses.

She focuses on the button and zip.

"I've never done this before," she says, almost to herself, and runs an experimental finger down my length. The first touch of her hand to my cock is electric, even though it's just a brush through a layer of fabric. I hiss with the effort required to hold back.

I hold my breath as she drags my boxers down. Not just because the cotton rubs my cock, but because I'm aware that what she's revealing is, shall we say, intimidating. Big. Thick and long.

"Oh!" She stares at my cock. "That's... Will it fit?"

"Yes." Because she was made for me. She might be small, but I have no doubt. "It'll hurt a bit the first time. And it'll always be tight, but I promise it will be worthwhile."

She nods. Her little hand cups around my length.

"That's it." A flex of my hips and she shifts her hand. An experimental stroke that feels simultaneously too much and not enough.

It's so slow that she brings her mouth to the rounded head. Pre-come beads at the top and the whole length throbs. Then blessed relief, her lips touch. A shudder goes through me. Her tongue slides out with deliberate languor, swishing over that droplet. She tastes me, pressing her lips together.

"You little tease," I growl as she draws back.

"You're salty, I knew you would be." She licks more

confidently this time, a broad sweep that sends sparks of pleasure right down to my balls. She explores me tentatively with her mouth and hand. Testing my hardness and easing her fingers around my girth. "How do I make you feel amazing?" she breaths onto my skin. "Teach me."

"Take me in your mouth." I can't keep in a grunt as she leans forwards further, her breasts pressing to my thighs and her forearms resting on my lap. "Suck."

I push her hair back when it falls over her face. I want to see her expression as she takes me in her mouth for the first time.

There's an infinite moment as she pushes the head of my cock between her plush lips. "Good girl. That's it."

She's hesitant at first, and the sight of her trying to figure out how to get more of me into her mouth is filthy as fuck.

"Up and down. It's most sensitive over the tip. Yeah like that, fuck but you're whip-smart," I add as she does as I say, her hand grasping at my leg.

She begins to bob her head, a sound of arousal and content from her throat. I've been dreaming of this, of her, and she is even better than I imagined. Sweet and intrigued and *willing*.

She's speeding up, getting into a rhythm, driving me right into craziness.

Oh fuck. I'm not going to last. She's so darn perfect. Except when her teeth catch me and I wince. Instantly she recognises the mistake and covers them, smoothing her hand up my side in apology.

Curious kitten that she is, her other hand eases down to my balls and she lets out a little whimper as she cups them.

"Is it their size you like?" They are big, and she nods. "The weight? They're full to bursting with seed just for you." That makes her redouble her efforts on my cock, the swollen head hitting the back of her throat. Her eyes are watering, but she's driving this, not me. She's swallowing further, harder, dirtier than I would have asked. But since she's offering, I'll fucking take it all. Particularly the submission of her sucking my cock like this. Her *choosing* to serve me. It's a powerful drug for us both. Me because I'm seeing her on her knees, sucking my cock just as I imagined when we first met. She's pleasuring me alone.

Her because she will only ever get complimented for this, and I'm at her mercy. I think she knows I'd do anything for her right now.

I might be hard as granite, but I'm putty in her hands.

"You're so good at this. The sight of your mouth around my cock is the sexiest thing I've ever seen. Your pink lips stretched. Those sounds you're making." Small whines of delight. "Your sweet tits just there for me to see bursting out of that dress."

Lacing my hand into her hair, the silky strands sliding over my knuckles, I encourage her. Show her the speed to tip me over.

The pressure builds and my balls tighten as she rubs them. I groan as I begin to lose control.

"I'm going to come. You don't want..." I try to pull her head from my cock. Partly because I don't want to shock her. The other aspect of my reluctance is far less honourable.

I want to see her marked as mine. My seed splattered over her creamy skin. On her face. Deep in her pussy, filling her to the point it drips out in a pretty mess. I want to breed her with babies who have my blue eyes and her straight dark hair.

She doesn't let me draw her away.

"Felicity." The pleasure overtakes me, fizzing down my back. I spurt into her mouth and she mews as it hits the back of her throat. My first orgasm since I jerked myself harshly in the car just after meeting her.

I should just accept this gift, but I'm a greedy bastard. I shove backwards and grab my cock. A line of spit curves between her lip and my shaft as I stroke through the last of my orgasm. Right onto her chest. Over the swell of her breasts, falling stark and white on the black of the dress.

Her throat bobs as she swallows, and that, along with seeing her covered with my mark, heightens the pleasure.

We both breathe hard, watching each other's eyes for a long moment as the tremors of coming fall away. I'm half expecting her to change her mind, feel bad perhaps. Have doubts.

"So." She sits back and gives me a cheeky grin, even as her eyes are shining with pride at having unravelled me. "I'd better have this dress, right?"

I roll my eyes, barely able to think past the post-orgasm bliss. Despite how intense that was, there's still a scratch. I need to fuck her. I have to fill her up, gushing wet heat while wedged deep inside her. But there's time.

I rally my thoughts. "How am I ever going to get you naked, and under me, if you own all these clothes?"

"You could take them off? Might be fun."

"I could rip them off. Then we'd end up back here next week, and the week after, and the one after that, with you trying on clothes and showing me your delectable body in infinite variations of pretty wrapping." That sounds like a great idea to me and the way she presses her thighs together suggests she thinks so too.

"That one we'll take, but it's a bit dirty. Is it available in white?" That would suit my purpose very nicely and save us another stop on our way north.

She tilts her head and rises to her feet. At the rack she finds the white version of the dress and holds it up, considering. It's slinky and long, with a slit up the side almost to her hip. "I can have this one too?"

I pretend to consider, pinching my eyebrows together as I do up my trousers.

"Cara, you can have *everything*."

10

FELICITY

I love him.

This should be insane. My rational brain is pointing out all the reasons this ought to be wrong, but it's not. It's *so right*. Every part of me has known rejection and hurt and heartbreak. I've spent years being unwanted. It's been an itchy, too tight, bobbled dress I've worn so long I didn't realise how it made me feel.

But that does mean I recognise how different being with Marco is.

Being with Marco isn't just having taken off that ill-fitting dress. It's like the clothes he bought me: perfectly fitted, soft and luxurious.

And it was that feeling which made me want to pleasure him, not the gifts.

I've heard about blow jobs, and been the subject of crude gestures and jokes. But being on my knees for him was a thrill of power. He broke apart for me, a girl who nobody thought was special.

And I saw the savage look in his eyes as he covered my breasts with his come. It was claiming, yes, but it was vulnerable too. At that moment I knew I could ask for anything and he'd do it, not just to have the moment of sexual bliss again, but to please me.

Afterwards he kept saying yes. Never impatient, never annoyed that I wanted something. We came away with bags of clothes and underwear that whenever they touch my skin, I'll remember the heat of his attention.

We have hours in the limo driving north to chat. I lean against him and answer his questions about cupcake recipes and decoration. He tells me about his work, pausing at the more unsavoury aspects, but continuing when I nod, unfazed. You don't live in a mafia compound all your life without seeing some darkness, and god knows it wasn't like there was anyone to protect me.

Until now. Marco seems intent on looking after me. He feels free to touch my body now, curling a strand of my hair around his finger or tucking it behind my ear. His hands are on me constantly. A stroke of my cheek, holding my waist.

We stop for an excessive lunch at a country hotel, with so many courses I lose track. I'm wearing the cut-off denim shorts and cami from earlier, along with cute canvas-top sneakers, and I'd probably have felt underdressed. Except I was with Marco, and he has this presence that says, *Do not fuck with me, you'd regret it.* And no one even looks askance at me.

Back in the car, it's like he can't decide what he wants to look at more as I speak. His gaze flits between my face, my legs, the place where the delicate top meets my breasts. And if that sounds carnal and greedy, well. I'm worse. I'm trying to cram a lifetime of memories into this journey. I catalogue his every feature, from his excessively long eyelashes to the silver in his curly hair.

"You can ask," he says eventually when I'm running my finger down his cheek again, skirting the scar.

"About...?"

He huffs.

Right. The scar. I'm curious, naturally, about how it happened. But that turns out not to be the question I care about most. "Does it hurt?"

"Not anymore, though it's a bit sensitive."

I press a kiss to his cheek, right over the scar, then check if he's okay with that. He's watching me, wary and still as a predator showing its underbelly.

"Who did it?"

"My father," he says calmly, a hint of amusement in his eyes. "He's already dead. By my hand."

Good. I don't reply because my jaw clenches so hard I might have to have it surgically re-opened. How dare that... I struggle to think of the right word. Bastard. Fucker. Cock-twat-douchbag. How dare anyone have harmed *my* man. Marco.

"You look positively murderous," he teases. "Do I need to dig him up so you can kill him again?"

I slap Marco's chest lightly, pouting. *"Yes.* We'll do it annually."

His chin tips up and he gives a growling purr. It's only then I realise what I've said. I've implied we'll be together. For years.

A sign for Carlisle flashes past.

That's close to Scotland, isn't it?

Oh no. No no no no no.

My tummy goes heavy, like I've eaten too much uncooked cake mixture. This is worse than getting salmonella poisoning. I cling to Marco.

"It won't be like that for our kids," he murmurs as he strokes my hair. "They'll have a good dad, I promise."

My eyes are hot and dry. I should just accept whatever happens. But I can't. I'm done with letting anyone determine my fate. I dig my nails into my palm as I look into his face.

"What's going on? What's the plan when we get to Scotland?" See, I can be brave.

"Isn't it obvious?" He quirks one eyebrow up, those blue eyes like the reflection of a blue-sky white water.

"No!" I'm brittle, caramelised sugar breaking into pieces as it cools. Stretched and changed by being with this man, I can't return to my original state of boring white granules of sweetness after being sinuously bent and heated.

These conflicted signals from him. First he says I'm his and makes me come so hard I nearly cracked a tooth, then he's taking me to Scotland. "What is all this for?"

He smooths his thumb over my lips. "We're going to Gretna Green."

I have definitely misheard. I'm losing my mind, because I could swear he just said we're going to Gretna Green.

"Why?" I croak.

"You want to be married, correct?"

How does he know that? I look away, out of the window. I can't bear for him to see how much I need this, because this is a cruel joke. It must be. The entirety of what I want does not just appear. That happens to... I dunno. No one. Girls in Regency romances, maybe. Or dogs, because all they want is a squeaky toy and a bowl of dog biscuits.

People like me don't get handsome men who adore and want to marry them. Green fields blur past and dappled light shines through the trees in their summer finery.

Marco grasps my chin uncompromisingly, hard enough to hurt, and forces it up so I have to meet his eyes.

"I know about what happened between your parents. How she fell for him and he abused that love. How he used her, and never married her, didn't give her the respect she deserved."

"How—"

"It's my business to make you happy, cara. That means I had to know about you. My entire team worked on Operation *Wife*. Paulo nearly gave the game away," he adds wryly. "Whisky, indeed. I know you didn't get the recognition a mafia princess should, or the love. All that ends today. As my wife, you'll have everything."

The shock is biting into a plain cupcake and finding delicious lemon curd filling. He knows all this—that I was unwanted and unnamed—and his answer is to give me his surname. Marriage. As clear a commitment as I could ask for.

"I can't bring back your mother." He shakes his head regretfully, not saying what we both know. She's dead. If she wasn't, she'd have come for me. "Your father was a petty, insecure, cruel man who couldn't cope with a woman who challenged him as your mother did. I could have stopped Westminster from murdering him, but I think he deserved it."

"I do too," I whisper.

My heart throbs. There's just one question I have to know the answer to before I say anything about marriage. "Was it you?"

11

MARCO

It depends what she means.

When I don't reply immediately she adds, "The book, chocolates, the card. And the... Ring."

Fingers crossed for foolhardy, but I won't lie to her. Even if my obsession could scare her away for good. "Yes."

"You were following me?"

How to explain the visceral need to see her, to be with her, to keep my girl safe? It's been a constant tug at my chest since we met, leading me to her.

I don't attempt to say all that. I simply nod.

"Stalking me."

I think of the CCTV cameras in her father's house that I hacked into. There wasn't anything too private, I'll give the bastard credit for that at least. Just corridors, public areas, and the kitchen. I liked watching Felicity in her kitchen. My baking queen.

"You could put it like that."

She licks her lips. How is it even legal for a girl to be this pretty?

I wait for the disgust, or judgement. Or perhaps the

next question: *Why*. She shoots a look at me from beneath long black lashes and I see the words in her eyes.

I'm willing to lay out my heart for her. I love her. I'm certain we belong together.

"Thank you for the gifts," she says instead.

"I'm sorry you had to leave them all behind."

"Only the book. I ate the kisses…" She smiles ruefully.

"And the other gift?" My heart hammers in my chest. A diamond ring. Not exactly the most subtle gift I've ever given, even if it wasn't as expensive as what I'd have chosen. But I saw the longing on her face as she examined the jewellery that day and didn't care about anything but making her smile.

"Why did you give it to me?"

"Why do you think?" I quirk one eyebrow up and she blushes. We're both circling around the real question here.

"I couldn't wear it before… But… I could now…?"

"Would you like to?" My heart is bashing around my ribcage as though it's been tossed over a waterfall in a barrel.

She's digging eagerly into the seams of her hoody grabbed from where it was discarded earlier, and a cautious smile lifts the corners of her mouth. "If you'd like me to?"

"I would."

Then the ring is glinting in her palm.

I lift it and for the second time in as many days I'm kneeling at her feet in the back of the car. But instead of snapping her bonds, this time I'm taking her hands in mine. They're small and delicate. I stroke my thumb over her palm. Her mouth falls open into a little 'o' and her pupils go wide. Blown.

Mmm. My girl.

I slowly slip the ring over her fourth fingertip, holding her gaze all the time. It's borderline erotic, a fore echo of my taking her virginity, slipping my cock into her, and we both know it. The smooth unyielding metal and her soft skin. My cock twitches. I'm rock-hard again.

Sliding it further, curving over her finger, it reaches her second knuckle. I push, the slightest pressure. Then the ring is over the barrier and onto her finger, snug.

Her breasts, only just covered by that little top, are rising and falling with laboured breath and the bottom of her neck is tinged pink. This is the hottest moment of my life, and none of the apparent good bits are involved. Not my cock, not her pussy. Not even our tongues.

I had no idea that the mere act of putting my ring on her finger would make pre-come seep from my erection. I'm so ready to claim her in the other way.

She flexes her hand and looks at the ring, admiring it, a pleased smile on her face.

"It suits you. A beautiful diamond for a beautiful girl."

"Thank you." She takes a deep breath. "Can I have one more thing?"

I wait.

"A kiss," she finishes awkwardly, eyes darting away. "A proper first kiss."

"First?" My mind goes full of static. We haven't kissed? No, she's right.

"When you... Put your mouth on mine last night. It was my first kiss," she confesses in a rush.

"Oh cara. I'm sorry." Not that I was the first to kiss her. I'm positively gleeful about that. But she's so perfect. Her first kiss should have been all sweetness and—yes—love. Not a tumultuous mixture of desperate lust and the need to keep her quiet.

I surge up and onto the seat beside her. Then I steady, focussing on her. I want us both to remember this. I skim my fingers through her hair deliberately until I reach the back of her head, then plunge them into the silk. I draw her forwards until our lips almost brush, so close my skin tingles in anticipation. For a few breaths I relish this moment.

"Let's try that first kiss again, shall we?" I whisper, and she whimpers and nods.

The first brush of our lips is a shock, even though I'm expecting it. Her lips are plush and soft but there's electricity between us. I'm leisurely. Gentle presses and catches, not deepening the kiss until I hear her breath hitch and she reaches for me. Her hand finds my shoulder and grips tight. An anchor in the storm of our kiss.

Her lips fall open and I take the invitation, sliding my tongue into her mouth. She lets out a mew of delight as I stroke the inside of her lip.

Our hands are still joined, and as I hold her head I rub my thumb over the place where her palm and fingers meet, feeling my ring there. She's wearing this sign of our commitment, and even though no words were said, I know she understands the significance. Pride seeps through me, feeling that band of metal—a sort of collar of ownership—as I kiss her. I take her first kiss and make it mine.

And when the kiss gradually goes deeper, wilder, dirtier, I can't help but grin. Because my clever girl is a quick study. No sooner as I've shown her something that feels good, but she tries it on me. To devastating effect.

I touch my tongue to hers, she copies and arousal unfurls in my groin. I suck her lip and graze it with my teeth and she retaliates with a nip.

"So perfect. You're being such a good girl for me," I growl as she tries thrusting her tongue into my mouth. Her hand on my shoulder has begun to wander. No longer looking for just support, she's stoking our desire by kneading the muscles and pressing her thumb along the roughness of my unshaven jawline.

I kiss her with all the longing of weeks of wanting her by my side, and the intensity demanded by my aching cock. I've thought so many times of this moment, of her in my arms, my ring on her finger.

I have to have her, and she has to be my *wife*.

"Cara," I say, drawing back. "Marry me."

Her eyes go wide. "But..."

12

FELICITY

I'm drunk on his kisses and his presence. And that ring. But yeah, it feels too good to be true. I'm struggling to believe it. "You really want to be married?"

I thought men avoided marriage, tried to not get trapped.

He cups my jaw, stroking my cheek with his thumb.

"Given your parents' story, I thought this would be important. I'm showing you in the best way I can think of, that I'm in this. You're it for me. I didn't spend weeks of my life obsessing over getting you into my life and bed to walk away afterwards. When we met, your soul tugged on a thread to mine I hadn't ever seen. That thread reeled me to you, and I'll never let you go. I love you."

He feels that too? My heart bursts.

"If you didn't want to be mine, you shouldn't have run and made me chase you. You should have said no. It's too late now, I'm keeping you." He grins wolfishly. "And that means we'll be married today."

I gape. I didn't believe him when he said I was his, but he's serious. All my doubts melt, insubstantial as rice paper.

"I love you," I whisper back. And it feels momentous to confess that, and also enough. I trust him. I did last night when he rescued me, and when we played chase. When he caught me. "We don't have to get married, so long as we're together."

This thing that's been part of my dreams I suddenly have clarity about. Marriage wasn't what was missing for my mother. Love was. All that matters is my being with Marco, and that we love each other.

A smile as warm as a waft of vanilla from an oven spreads across Marco's face.

"I want to. I want you to be mine, permanently, and everyone to know. And I want you to know you are mine, with no doubt whatsoever."

There are no words to do justice to this moment, so instead I crawl across the short distance of seat and snuggle into his lap, my thighs over his. He tightens his arms around me, pulling me flush to him, the hard length of his cock pressing into my lower belly. Heat unfurls, bright and pleasurable.

He wants me.

And I want him, so what exactly am I waiting for? A divine sign of approval?

Who needs god if Marco will call me his good girl.

"Marco, I can't wait for marriage. Please. Now." I have to have him inside me, filling me.

I'm grasping at his belt before I can think through what I'm doing. It's no easier this time, apparently once is not enough to make me less fumbly, but I realise I have a bigger issue. My shorts.

Marco, my husband-to-be and absolute trooper, doesn't hesitate. He releases his cock without another word as I stand on wobbly legs. The movement of the limo threatens to unbalance me and so do my weak knees.

He reaches out a hand to steady me as we round a corner, at the same time he strokes his cock with the other and I'm hopelessly distracted by the sight of his big hand on his cock as I strip off the shorts, and the knickers we bought too, shimmying them down my legs.

"And your top." His voice is uncompromising.

I obey, and unclip my new bra too, tossing it aside and kneeling over his lap.

"I need you," I say around his kiss as he drags me closer and devours my lips. My knees dig into the seat and I writhe against the solid presence of my fiancé.

"Go on then," he murmurs between kissing down my neck, making his way to my breasts where he moans as he sucks first one nipple then the other into his mouth. "Use me. Fuck me. Make me come right up against your womb and breed you. You want that too, right?"

I nod desperately. Yes. Yes, that as well. Having a baby always felt further away than the moon, but with him? Yes.

"Take everything you need. I'm yours." He holds his cock in one hand and my squishy hip in the other and lines us up.

I lower myself, my dripping folds coming up against the immovable hardness of his erection. Already it a feeling of completeness. My pussy throbs. My clit, I dunno how, but I swear it bounces like an overexcited creature with its own will.

Bearing down is sweet torture. It's pressure and stretch and I hiss at the burn as I take his first inch.

"Yes. You're so brave, I know that hurts," he murmurs, his voice low and gruff. "Now more, because you feel like heaven to me."

He said to take him, but of course he's still in control of this, encouraging me as I slip another inch onto his cock. I'd think it wasn't possible, that we won't fit, but Marco doesn't leave any more room for that anxiety than he does space in my stretched-out pussy. There's no fear left anywhere. He has chased it all away with his love and his amazing big body.

The next inch is easier, so I slip down another, my thigh muscles creaking with the effort. The next is more difficult again, but now instead of holding still, Marco is thrusting from below. And each slow retreat takes him deeper as he slides back into me. So devious, my husband-to-be. He takes what he wants without asking.

And what he wants is—and this shocks the hell out of me, even after his declarations—me.

I try the same trick as him, rising up and lowering myself harder, trying to get him deeper.

"That's it, you're so good." He's holding me with both hands now, no need for his guidance to keep us together. "You're taking me perfectly. My good girl."

His praise lights me up. The reassurance that I'm doing this right, combined with the delicious hardness of him stretching me open is magic.

It takes several careful thrusts, working him into me, until he's sliding all the way with no friction. He's so deep I can feel him up to my belly button. I swear he rearranged all my internal organs for that massive cock of his. How do I even have room? He's filled a gap I didn't even know existed.

It wasn't there, obviously, otherwise he wouldn't have stretched me out. It was a gap that he had to prise open to reveal, a void of loneliness that is now full of him. Stuffed. And soon he'll spill wet heat into me, seed that will bind us together even more. Joining with Marco like this chases away the last tiny vestige of loneliness.

We're both moving faster now, getting savage and needy. He's gripping my hips to slam me down onto his cock and I'm holding his shoulders, supporting myself as best I can to meet the thrusts he's filling me with from below. He's a force of nature. A hurricane and I want all of him. Daily. Forget an apple to keep the doctor away, or a balanced diet, I'm having sex with Marco. His cock inside me is all the sustenance I need. There's no discomfort now. The feel of his cock sliding on my inner walls is fogging my mind.

He plunges his hand into my hair even as he slides his hold to my bottom, digging his fingers in so hard it might bruise. I don't care. I want his marks on me. He's so confident, I love it. I'm his to do with as he wishes, and he wants to fuck me. Spill inside me. Breed me, he said.

"Look."

I can't. I'm almost cross-eyed with pleasure.

He snarls at my disobedience and thrusts up, hard. I cry out at how deep and good he feels.

"Look," he orders again.

I follow his gaze to between our bodies. His cock is glistening with my arousal, stark skin surrounded by dark fabric. I've creamed all over him and it's obscenely hot against that pristine suit.

"See how well you're taking my fat cock?"

His cock disappears into me as I feel him thrust, and somehow seeing that at the same time as the pleasure spreads out from where I'm taking him makes this all the hotter. I thought nothing could feel as good as him inside me, but I was totally wrong. The sight of him sliding between my legs is better, spiking arousal that makes my clit pulse.

"Such a good fucking girl." He reaches between us and his thumb finds that bundle of nerves that respond better to his touch than anything else. I meet his gaze and it's implacable. "Now, cara," he says in a stern voice. "Come on my cock."

13

MARCO

She grips me with her cunt so intensely as she comes, I might pass out from the blood trapped in my cock. I hang onto her curves, tensing every muscle I have in me to prevent her from tipping me over too. Not yet. One orgasm is not enough for my girl on her first time. Two, absolute minimum, especially as she still owes me one of her orgasms for earlier in the boutique.

She's so sensitive to my every touch, alight with every stroke of my hands and every thrust. We're attuned to each other.

Fuck, she feels amazing. My perfect fit. This sweet, cupcake making, suspicious woman is my whole life now. Her pussy has demonic magic, so hot and tight I think it's eating me whole even as her orgasm ebbs away. Absolutely the best thing I've ever felt is her coming from my touch.

"You're mine. I'm not letting you go now," I tell her as she sags against my chest. "I'll stalk you to the ends of the earth if you try to leave. Wherever you go, I'll follow. Your dark shadow. I'm that addicted to you, and I'll make you addicted to me too."

She sounds like she already is, whimpering as her hair tickles my throat when she nods.

I've ruined her. She's practically boneless now and fun as it is to have her on top of me, I need more. Or rather, the possessive monster in me needs to take control, and isn't satisfied.

I want her on her back, beneath me, looking up as I cover her with my body and fill her. I'm still completely dressed, but for my cock poking obscenely from my trousers. When we're married there will be so many opportunities for us to be skin-to-skin, intimate. For now, I just need her to come again so I can release into her.

I hold her to me as I shift and lay her down along the padded bench seat, her naked skin creamy and freckled against the black leather. The movement draws me out nearly all the way, just the tip of my cock still in her. I drive in, hard, and she gasps, rolling her hips up.

"That's my good girl."

She whines in what I can only assume is agreement. Smiling as I settle into a rhythm that keeps me right on the edge of coming, I take her in. Hair a mess, spread around her head. Naked body exposed and writhing with renewed pleasure. I'll want this girl forever. There's no way I can get enough of her soft body and strawberry scent.

Her tits are way too tempting, falling a little to the side and jiggling as I thrust into her again and again. I lean down and bite that soft plump flesh gently, then not-so-gently as I hear her gasp and her pussy clenches around me. I worship her breasts and she writhes, offering herself to my dirty fantasies.

So damn pretty. Holding myself on one elbow so I can kiss her mouth, I lift her thigh, opening her up so I can go deeper.

"I love you. I'm going to have you in every way you can imagine and many you can't," I say between dirty kisses that she returns with tongue and teeth going wild. "On your hands and knees, your arse in the air. With your ankles at my shoulders. Riding me from behind as I stroke your back or cup your tits. I can't wait, cara. I'm going to defile you in the most delicious ways."

She clutches at me as I pump into her, her hips meeting mine, slapping our flesh together almost violently. Her fingers can't settle. They're in my hair, nails digging into my scalp and dragging down my back. Even through my shirt I can feel her intent to take a chunk out of me for herself. And that's fine by me. I'm hers.

And she is *mine*. I catch one of her hands, lacing our fingers together, and press it into the seat beside her head. Then the other. Having her pinned beneath me by my pistoning cock is primitive. Close and intimate despite my clothes. The sort of sex I dreamed of having with her.

I'm pounding her into the seat, out of control and animalistic. My head is full of possessive lust and the need to paint her with my seed. To come deep inside her so she's pregnant with my child after this. To breed her.

It's not just the unimaginable pleasure of her tight virgin pussy, although that's like nothing I've ever felt before. It's the feeling of owning my girl, of having her completely, and watching her pleasure. Her fingers grip the back of my hands where I'm pressing her down. And after weeks of being apart from her, the creature in my chest that wanted to drag her to its lair is purring. I'm staring into her grey eyes, seeing her lose herself in pleasure I've given her, spearing her with my cock and holding her hands in mine, palm to palm. Those eyes of hers are beautiful, full of white stars I fall into.

I can't believe I'm this lucky. She's perfect and amazing. I tell her in broken phrases how she's my world. That I love her and I'm going to care for her and fuck her and give her orgasms every day. And my girl smiles as she pants and whines, so close to coming.

"I'm going to spoil you," I grind out the promise, still looking into her eyes. I want her to see when I spill into her. "I'll give you all of me. Every drop of my come until you're overflowing with it, wrecked and dirty. But I'm going to take as well. Your virginity is already mine, but I'm ravenous. I'll have all you give me and more. I'll take your pleasure, and steal my own, using your pussy and your mouth. I'll make you my sweet, cherished whore as well as my wife. Everything. I'll have to be inside you more times a day than you can take."

"I can take it," she gasps out. "Anything you give, everything you want, Marco."

I growl. That's the answer I didn't know I needed. She'll give me *everything*.

And in return, I grant the release she's desperately seeking. I reach down, cramming my hand between our bodies and not letting up on the hard thrusts. My fingers find her clit, and I stroke her.

Once, twice, and she shatters. She grips my cock even tighter than before, milking me. And I didn't mean for this to end—god knows I'd have kept fucking her until the end of time, I love being inside her that much—but she drags me over with her into hot spurt after hot spurt.

I keep coming, more than I can remember. I've been waiting for her and my body knows what its job is here: to breed her.

It's with primal delight I feel the wetness overflowing,

making us both sticky. All that seed for my girl, and a baby soon too.

She giggles and hides her wide grin when we pull up outside the famous blacksmiths in Gretna Green. The sunset stains the sky red and purple, and the yellow evening light catches on Felicity's white dress, making it gold like the decorations she used to warn me the first time we met.

She changed into that flowing dress when I finally conceded she'd had enough orgasms for now. I allowed a slight clean-up, but I know for a fact my semen is still dripping through her knickers and down the inside of her thigh, and I'm glad. I want everyone to smell sex on her, and know she belongs to me.

"I can't believe we're really going to get married at Gretna Green today," she says as I help her out of the limo and she straightens her white dress.

"Do you mind?"

"No." She wraps an arm around my waist. "I like that you know what you want."

"And what I want is you." I pull her in with a hand on her shoulder. She fits me perfectly.

"It's like a romance novel," she marvels as we take in the little whitewashed cottage.

"You wanted to be married to a Regency rake, didn't you?"

"A duke, actually."

"Brat," I reply affectionately. I love her sassy mouth. "You got kidnapped by a..." I'm distracted by her hand sliding down to the top of my arse.

"I think you count as a highwayman?"

"Right, a highwayman. That will have to do, as I have no intention of letting you go."

"Oh thank god, because I suspect I'd die without you."

"Mr Brent." A man meets us at the door with a nod. I owe Paulo a pay raise I decide, as I find he's fixed all the paperwork so I don't have to threaten to kill anyone because they don't deal with getting us married quickly enough, as well as arranged nice touches like a bouquet and champagne that make the stars in Felicity's eyes sparkle even brighter.

The ceremony is thankfully short, which is good because I'm impatient to have Felicity in my arms and on my cock again. There are vows that I repeat, promises to love no matter what. And when she says the same to me, my heart expands so big it threatens to crack my ribs from the inside. She slides a ring onto my finger and we smirk at each other at the symbolism and the memories. There is going to be so much time for us to make all the tender and wild moments together. The rest of our lives.

We retire to a hotel and it's after I've got her back into bed and enjoyed my white-clad bride that we're lying on the bed, her laid over me, that she brings it up. We've talked about some of our future, each feeling out the other's preferences. I just say yes to whatever she wants. Eight kids? Sure. Another library? Why not. A bakery? Why not two?

"What about Westminster?"

"What about them?"

"Won't they still be after me? They were pretty intent on wiping out Kensington."

I pull out my phone.

"How do you have this number?" the kingpin of Westminster, Benedict Crosse, snaps.

"Hello to you too, Crosse." I get distracted by Felicity's

ankle, bending her knee so it's closer, stroking over the bone and pressing into her achilles.

I only realise I've been silent when my neighbouring mafia lord says irritably, "What do you want?"

"If anything happens to Kensington's daughter, I will consider it as a personal attack." Her whole foot fits in my hand. It's dainty and I massage the arch, making her sigh happily.

"Oh that was you, was it?" he drawls. "I wondered who took the girl."

"*My* girl." I transfer my attention to the ball of her foot. I'll need to do her other foot too. "My *wife*."

"Mmm. She's inherited a lot of debt." Crosse's last word is clipped and threatening.

"And you're going to wipe it off her record, or I'll be offering that university student who visits you *a job*. Your son's girlfriend, I believe?" Two can play at threats to young women under the care of mafia bosses. I have an extensive spy network, and I know about Crosse's soft spot for the girl.

There's a long, tense silence.

"Fine," Benedict spits, then hangs up.

"All sorted." I toss my phone away and pull Felicity up to kiss me again. "Now, what else would my wife like?"

EPILOGUE
MARCO

6 YEARS LATER

The scent of vanilla and the ring of laughter draws me away from work. I follow my nose and lean in the doorway to the kitchen. My wife and daughters are baking.

Felicity leaves her bakery early on a Friday and spends the afternoon with our twin troublemakers before we travel up to Scotland to spend the weekend in our other family home.

"Less eating the icing, Maeve, or there won't be any left for the cakes," Felicity says, taking a batch of cupcakes from the oven.

Sophie and Maeve look at one another. They're wearing identical outfits, little white dresses with red polka dots that if I didn't know better I'd say were reminiscent of cherries. My wife has a naughty sense of humour and loves to remind me of when our babies were conceived.

"How does she know without even looking? She's magical," I say. Two pairs of bright silver eyes swivel to me and there's the screech of chairs as they both throw themselves out of their seats and race around the table to clutch my knees.

"Daddy, Daddy! Pick us up!"

"Pick me up first!" Sophie demands.

"You're getting too big for this." Leaning down I grab them both up simultaneously, one in each arm, gripped to my sides. They're still not heavy, but I like to tease them a bit.

"Never too big," Maeve whispers, pressing a sticky kiss to my cheek. They love sugar, my girls. Almost as much as I do. I've discovered a sweet tooth since I met Felicity.

"Never," I agree, kissing her on her dark curly-haired head. I had a bet with Felicity that they would get my eyes.

Yeah. Expensive call.

Not that it mattered. I can afford anything she wants. I still run Brent, and it remains the inky shadow of the London mafias. Darker, quieter, more likely to swallow you whole. But with a little less direct involvement from me than I used to demand. Paulo relishes his expanded position, and frankly has earned it. And in turn, I adore spending time with my wife and family.

Scaring my enemies is still fun, don't get me wrong, but I prefer my two little terrors.

"Right, are you two going to decorate these cakes with me, or what?"

There's yells and squeals of approval as I carry my giggling daughters over to the table where Felicity is waiting, a wry smile on her face. It amuses her how indulgent I am of our kids.

"Hello, cara." I lean in and kiss my beautiful wife, and she sighs with happiness.

"Daddy! Cupcakes!" Sophie complains when Felicity and my kiss goes on longer than she thinks it should.

"Later," I promise Felicity as I pull away, kick out a chair, and settle the girls on my lap.

I scoop over cupcakes and a piping bag of icing. The three of us decorate our cakes. Under my daughters' watchful eyes and with their directions, I do most of the tricky piping of the buttercream. Felicity contentedly decorates the remaining cakes in her signature elegant style and putters around the kitchen. She loves to just have me and the kids with her, enjoying the things she loves.

With bright coloured hundreds and thousands and every decoration on the table, Sophie is an agent of chaos. Nothing is too pink or too much. Maeve is more thoughtful, but still has the instincts of a little girl, making her cake also very pink, if more restrained. They both eat an obscene amount of the sugary decorations. The jelly lemon and orange slices are a favourite for eating, if not for putting on their cakes. Me? I prefer the ripe red fruits Felicity always puts out. Raspberries and strawberries from Scotland, soft and sweet and just a tiny bit sharp. Fragrant, and they go ideally with vanilla.

I try to keep my cupcake simple, though I know it's a failing mission. Both girls delight in piling decorations onto mine when I'm not looking, which makes Felicity laugh behind her hand.

When at last all of our cupcakes look as though a decoration tornado has hit, I say, "Are we ready? We're ready!"

"Who is going to win this time?" Felicity comes around behind us and looks over my shoulder. This is part of our tradition: she judges the cake decoration with her expert eye.

"It's mine! Mine is the best!" Sophie shrieks right in my ear, and I wince.

"Certainly you're the loudest," I mutter.

"Mmmm. This one has lovely colours," Felicity says, pointing at Sophie's cake. She finds something to praise on each of the cakes. Even mine. "I love this pattern here," she adds, pointing at Maeve's swirl of red.

"I think..." She leaves a long pause, like we're contestants on a television baking show. "Daddy's is the best."

Maeve and Sophie let out twin exasperated groans of, "Oh Mummy!"

I cackle as I lift my daughters off my knees and stand to claim my prize. Where Sophie or Maeve get extra time on their preferred games or credit towards whatever they're saving up for, I get my favourite reward.

"No more kissing, it's yukky!" Sophie complains.

"Alright, we'll save my prize for later," I say, and Felicity smiles. "Let's get this cleared up and let's have some dinner."

The girls hurry to help.

I pick up the last of the buttercream we used to decorate the cakes. "I'll be taking this."

Felicity's eyes go wide. Because she knows what that means. She knows how I like to eat buttercream icing.

EXTENDED EPILOGUE
MARCO

6 YEARS LATER, THAT EVENING

Our bedroom is dark and silent when I come from the bathroom, and I smile.

Of all the games we play, this might be my favourite. My good girl, she knows how to earn her orgasms with the acts I need almost as much as she does.

You'd think after years of marriage and two kids that we'd have tailed off in our desire for each other and kinky sex with each other. But no. Though we don't have quite the insatiable appetites that we did before the twins were born, we take every opportunity and make time to quickly satisfy ourselves against walls, in cupboards, or more luxuriously, in bed once the babies are asleep.

I pad into the bedroom and admire my wife. Felicity has been everything to me since we met, and the soft light of a table lamp left on spreads warmth over her naked uncovered shoulders and neck. She's on her front, hair spilling over the pillow and eyes closed.

My cock stirs at the sight of her bare skin. I want to bite her. Consume her.

I give myself a lazy stroke and think about how I'm going to fuck my sweet wife. On my bedside cabinet is the bowl of buttercream icing from earlier. Sweet and soft and good, just like her. I don't know what I'm looking forward to more.

Fully hard, I approach the bed, pausing at my bedside cabinet for a single thin piece of plastic, then slip beneath the covers. But I don't settle down for the night, even though Felicity's even breaths suggest she's sleeping. Straddling her, I put my hand over her mouth and slide my knee between hers. Too easily her legs part.

She's awake, of course she is.

"Tap, tap, tap," I murmur as I grab her hands and pull them above her head. A reminder of her safe signal. Three taps and I stop everything. Her foot. Her fingers. Anything. Never happened yet, but I won't forget to remind my girl that she is safe with me.

She struggles and tugs as I secure her wrists with a zip tie, and I feel her fast pulse under my fingertips. She's so fragile and yet so vibrant.

"What are you—" she hisses with faux outrage.

"Shhh. Don't want to wake the kids, do you? That would be dangerous." She's lying on her front and hell, but she knows the feel of her peachy arse against my cock makes me ravenous. I cup her pussy, her cream wetting my hand. Fuck, but we both enjoy this a little too much. "Be a good quiet girl."

"Make me."

I thought my dick couldn't get any harder, but I was wrong. So very wrong.

Pressing one hand over her mouth, I force myself closer

between her legs and position the head of my throbbing cock at her entrance.

The grunt of approval is instinctive and unbidden as I find her soaking wet. "You were thinking about this, weren't you, you dirty girl."

I feel her nod.

"Were you thinking about a strange man coming and taking you in your bed? Your stalker."

This time it's a whine of pure need and she pushes herself back onto my cock, getting just the tip inside before I pull back with a huff of laughter.

"Slutty little wife wants cock, huh?" I cover her body with mine, letting my weight settle onto her as she's told me she likes. My girl likes to feel my strength, to be forced and overpowered. Pushing her into the mattress in a prelude of what's to come. Me pounding her in with my cock. "Do you need to be taken, dark and filthy?"

She's shaking with the combination of pleasure, desire and the hint of fear.

"Doesn't matter what you want though, does it?" I grip her thigh and yank her up so she's completely open to me. I smooth my palm over that soft skin.

"I'm going to take whatever I want. You love that. You enjoy me stealing what I want from you, no asking. And what I want, cara, is this tight pussy around my cock."

She moans as I tease us both, pressing and withdrawing, but never slipping all the way into her.

"I'm going to violate you," I breathe and yeah, she likes that word too. "You're so wet, my good quiet girl. So perfect and willing, whatever you protest."

She's impossibly drenched, creaming all over the tip of my cock, and it's that more than anything else that works me up into a frenzy.

"Cara, I'm going to fuck you into submission."

With that last word, I thrust into her.

Violently.

She bucks at my sudden invasion and I choke on the tight grip on my cock, my heart being ripped out of my chest with duelling instincts. I want to pause and avoid giving her pain, fuck into her again because it feels like heaven, and remove my hand to ask if she's okay and hear her voice saying she wants more.

I thrust again. Harder, but not so hard I don't feel her wiggle into this, trying to get the angle just right.

Fuck, she's perfect. I give up and pound into her. I don't hold back. My balls slap her clit and my hips bang into her arse. I hit the end of her passage, and damn but it feels amazing combined with her cream leaking over my cock. She takes everything I give her as I unleash all the desperate need I've built up since we last made love. Because even as I'm brutal, holding her down, fucking into her, I am aware that much as I'm claiming her body with every possessive thrust, she owns my heart.

I'm hers as much as she is mine.

Probably more.

"You're accepting my big cock so well," I whisper, not stopping in the punishing rhythm. "Quiet good girls get rewarded with their clits stroked."

That nod and whimper. It makes my heart clench even as I reach around her thigh and find her clit.

It doesn't take much. Just my fingers rubbing the swollen little bud in small circles, the exact speed and pressure that I know gets her off every time.

She turns her head into the pillow as she comes, screaming. It takes my hand and the pillow to muffle her cries to an acceptable volume, and I keep moving through it all. Her clenching. The way she's squeezing my cock.

"That's it, my best girl," I sooth her as the convulsions ebb away. "You want me to come inside you, don't you, cara? Coming on my cock like that so perfectly, you nearly tipped me over too."

There's a tremble in her shoulders beneath me.

My brat. She's laughing.

Pulling out abruptly, I release her mouth and sit onto my heels.

"On your back," I snarl, and she hastens to obey, wriggling her pretty body over, because her hands are still trapped above her head. "Much as I love your perfect arse, I want to fuck you and see those pert breasts of yours."

She lets out a whimper and flexes her torso, inviting me. Her tits are even more lovely than when we first met, a richer diet and two children having made her softer and rounder. I love the little roll at her belly, and the way her tits fall into my palms now as I cup them. She moans as I swipe my thumbs over her nipples, back and forth, watching her face contort with pleasure. When I lean over her and press our lips together, the kiss goes messy, feral, immediately. Her mouth is open to me, her pants a little jagged as she struggles to contain her arousal as I kiss her everywhere. Her cheeks, her lips. I adore kissing her neck too.

But my cock is still a throbbing demanding bar, so I shift back and take a moment to admire the view, stroking my cock lazily. It's sticky with her cream, and though there's nothing as good as sinking into her, I love the anticipation too.

"Enjoy that, huh?"

"Yes," she whispers, a satisfied smile playing around her mouth and a gleam in her eyes.

"More?"

"Give me your come."

I nod slowly. "Over your tits perhaps. Make a filthy girl of you." I brush my fingers over said breasts, then lean forwards, stroking over her neck, pausing to show her how my hand encompasses it. "Or here?" I flick my forefinger up to her jawline. "All over your pretty face."

She licks her lips and her breathing is quick and shallow even though I haven't restricted it in the slightest. Her gaze bounces down to where I'm easing my hand over my cock.

Ah, yes of course.

"Or do you want it here." I trail my hand down towards me, then pause as my fingertips rest on her mons and the heel of my hand is at her entrance. "Deep in here, yes? Where I'll breed you."

"Please," she begs in a breathy undertone. "Fill me up."

I pull her arse onto my lap, spreading her legs and lifting one of her ankles to my shoulder as I do so. I love having her so exposed. Her pink folds are slick and it's the best sight. This time I slide in easily, having fucked her loose.

I know how to make her clench and tight around me. Reaching for her clit so quickly after her last orgasm risks it being sore, but she keens, shutting her eyes and stretching out her bound hands above her as I begin to touch her and fuck her deeply at the same time.

She's spread across my lap, impaled on my cock, her arms over her head, completely naked. I'm the luckiest man alive. I hold her with one hand, firm enough to bruise and I haven't moved on from wanting to mark her as mine, so yeah, I really like pulling her onto my cock like this. My other hand strokes her clit, and this view is better every time we do this. Her pale skin scattered with freckles, those rosy nipples. I'm just as obsessed as I was when we first met. Worse, perhaps, because every orgasm I watch her have makes her more beautiful to me. Maybe it's just because she feels closer, like she belongs to me more thoroughly every time I'm the reason she comes.

And she's about to again, as I keep thrusting into her, taking my own pleasure. We play this game that I'm forcing her and using her body, but the truth is there's nothing for me without knowing she's getting off on what I'm doing to her.

A damn good thing it's the same things that make her wet and me hard. But it's not surprising. Every game we play comes down to one simple element: I want to own her and care for her, and she wants to be mine.

"Be my very good girl and come again on your husband's cock, cara," I growl.

She keeps watching me, those stunning silver eyes lingering as I circle over his clit faster and harder until she orgasms on my cock, thrashing and jerking, coming so strongly it looks like it almost hurts in the best way.

This time, the feeling of rolling clenches along with seeing her face squeezes pleasure from my balls to the tip of my cock.

I come with a groan, so hard I swear my soul leaves my body along with all that semen. I fill her up, spurt after spurt, deep inside her. Ream after ream goes into her, right up against her cervix. Right where it's most needed. It's magic, and I growl, "Going to get you pregnant again, cara."

"Yes. Breed me," she murmurs, so utterly sated from her orgasms she's slurring.

I hold her leg to my chest, pressing my lips to the arch of her foot as the spasms of pleasure that shake me finally subside.

We stay like that for long minutes, until I finally have to pull out. There's a gush of our joint wetness from her pink hole, and I grin as I reach for the buttercream icing from the bedside cabinet. With my right hand, I scoop the sweet treat from the bowl and smear it onto my wife's deliciously soft belly. She watches, knowing eyes attempting to be innocent. "What are you doing?"

"Making you dessert."

With my left hand, I stroke along her thigh, gently caressing her until I reach her pussy. Then I dive my fingers right in, slipping two fingers into her messy passage. Sometimes I make her squeeze her thighs together and keep my come in her, but tonight I coax her legs open and enjoy the sloppy texture of her soft dripping pussy.

"Such a dirty girl," I chastise lovingly as my fingers are covered with my seed and her cream. Then I wipe that combination of juices over her breasts, going back to smear on more, and more again. "Want a taste?"

"Yes, sir."

"You'll make me hard again, saying that," I say with amusement, and she grins.

"Oh no," she deadpans. "Not round two with my sexy gorgeous husband. Not in one night. What a terrible thing."

"Shush, brat." I dab my buttercream covered fingers into the come I've spread on her belly and stretch out my arm. "Open your lips and swallow your husband's come."

She lifts herself to my fingers and lines up her mouth. As her tongue touches my fingers, then envelopes them, my cock twitches. There will never be a day I don't want Felicity.

I feed her all the buttercream like that. She sucks my fingers and swirls her tongue around to get every drop. It's a heady combination, the icing, the sweetness of her cream, and the salt and musk of my come. A little protein on the side, right?

That mouth of hers. I love it in all the ways she serves me. Around my cock is a favourite of course, but this is just as delicious in another way. I feed her and tease that she's a hungry little slut and she just nods and opens her mouth.

"You did so well," I say when she's lapped up everything I've offered and I snip the zip tie with scissors left in the bedside cabinet for that purpose. I check her wrists and kiss all over her petite hands.

She collapses back onto the pillows, exhausted and happy. Her eyes are closed when I return from the bathroom with a washcloth and clean her up, leaving kisses as I pat her tummy dry. Those stretch marks from pregnancy are almost as good as the light bruises. Maybe I like them more, actually. They're womanly, and nothing says I belong to my husband like the lines that show she was pregnant by me.

When I'm done, I snap the lights off and settle onto the bed beside Felicity. She snuggles in. I pull her into my arms and stroke her hair, her neck, and brush her cheek with the side of my thumb. I keep smoothing my palm over her until she's fast asleep, nestled into me, and I'm full of the satisfaction of having pleased the most important person in my life.

Then my hand stills on her neck, resting possessively on her beating pulse. And my eyelids drop in the darkness. Relaxed and sleepy on top of me, she's yet another variation of perfect.

So peaceful. Unutterably content. In love.

We're both where we belong as I fall into slumber. With each other.

THANKS

Thank you for reading, I hope you enjoyed it.

Want to read a little more Happily Ever After? Click to get exclusive epilogues and free stories! or head to EvieRoseAuthor.com

If you have a moment, I'd really appreciate a review wherever you like to talk about books. Reviews, however brief, help readers find stories they'll love.

Love to get the news first? Follow me on your favored social media platform - I love to chat to readers and you get all the latest.

If the newsletter is too much like commitment, I recommend following me on BookBub, where you'll just get new release notifications and deals.

- amazon.com/author/evierose
- bookbub.com/authors/evie-rose
- instagram.com/evieroseauthor
- tiktok.com/@EvieRoseAuthor

INSTALOVE BY EVIE ROSE

Stalker Kingpins

Spoiled by my Stalker

From the moment we lock eyes, I'm his lucky girl... But there's a price to pay

Owned by her Enemy

I didn't expect the ruthless new kingpin—an older man, gorgeous and hard—to extract such a price for a ceasefire: an arranged marriage.

His Public Claim

My first time is sold to my brother's best friend

Pregnant by the Mafia Boss

Kingpin's Baby

I beg the Kingpin for help... And he offers marriage.

Baby Proposal

My boss walked in on me buying "magic juice" online... And now he's demanding to be my baby's daddy!

Grumpy Bosses

Older Hotter Grumpier

My billionaire boss catches me reading when I should be working. And the punishment...?

Tall, Dark, and Grumpy

When my boss comes to fetch me from a bar, I'm expecting him to go nuts that I'm drunk and described my fake boyfriend just like him. But he demands marriage...

London Mafia Bosses

Captured by the Mafia Boss

I might be an innocent runaway, but I'm at my friend's funeral to avenge her murder by the mafia boss: King.

Taken by the Kingpin

Tall, dark, older and dangerous, I shouldn't want him.

Stolen by the Mafia King

I didn't know he has been watching me all this time.

I had a plan to escape. Everything is going perfectly at my wedding rehearsal dinner until *he* turns up.

Caught by the Kingpin

The kingpin growls a warning that I shouldn't try his patience by attempting to escape.

There's no way I'm staying as his little prisoner.

Claimed by the Mobster

I'm in love with my ex-boyfriend's dad: a dangerous and powerful mafia boss twice my age.

Snatched by the Bratva

I have an excruciating crush on this man who comes into the coffee shop. Every day. He's older, gorgeous, perfectly dressed. He has a Russian accent and silver eyes.

Kidnapped by the Mafia Boss

I locked myself in the bathroom when my date pulled out a knife. Then a tall dark rescuer crashed through the door... and kidnapped me.

Held by the Bratva

"Who hurt you?"

Before I know it, my gorgeous neighbour has scooped me up into his arms and taken me to his penthouse. And he won't let me go.

Seized by the Mafia King

I'm kidnapped from my wedding

Filthy Scottish Kingpins

Forbidden Appeal

He's older and rich, and my teenage crush re-surfaces as I beg the former kingpin to help me escape a mafia arranged marriage. He stares at me like I'm a temptress he wants to banish, but we're snowed in at his Scottish castle.

Captive Desires

I was sent to kill him, but he's captured me, and I'm at his mercy. He says he'll let me go if I beg him to take his...

Eager Housewife

Her best friend's dad is advertising for a free use convenient housewife, and she's the perfect applicant.